5th Judgement

JAMES PATTERSON is one of the best-known and biggest-selling writers of all time. He is the author of some of the most popular series of the past decade – the Alex Cross, Women's Murder Club and Detective Michael Bennett novels – and he has written many other number one bestsellers including romance novels and stand-alone thrillers. He lives in Florida with his wife and son.

James is passionate about encouraging children to read. Inspired by his own son who was a reluctant reader, he also writes a range of books specifically for young readers. James has formed a partnership with the National Literacy Trust, an independent, UK-based charity that changes lives through literacy. In 2010, he was voted Author of the Year at the Children's Choice Book Awards in New York.

For more information about James Patterson's novels, visit
www.jamespatterson.co.uk

Or become a fan on Facebook

9th Judgement

James Patterson

WITH MAXINE PAETRO

arrow books

Published in the United Kingdom by Arrow Books in 2011

3 5 7 9 10 8 6 4 2

Copyright © James Patterson, 2010

James Patterson has asserted his right under the Copyright, Designs and
Patents Act, 1988 to be identified as the author of this work

First published in Great Britain in 2010 by
Century

Arrow Books
Random House, 20 Vauxhall Bridge Road,
London SW1V 2SA

www.rbooks.co.uk

Addresses for companies within The Random House Group Limited
can be found at: www.randomhouse.co.uk/offices.htm

The Random House Group Limited Reg. No. 954009

A CIP catalogue record for this book
is available from the British Library

ISBN 9780099525387
ISBN 9780099549529 (export edition)

The Random House Group Limited supports The Forest Stewardship
Council (FSC), the leading international forest certification
organisation. All our titles that are printed on Greenpeace approved FSC
certified paper carry the FSC logo. Our paper procurement policy can be
found at www.rbooks.co.uk/environment

Mixed Sources
Product group from well-managed
forests and other controlled sources
www.fsc.org Cert no. TT-COC-2139
© 1996 Forest Stewardship Council
FSC

Typeset by SX Composing DTP, Rayleigh, Essex
Printed and bound in Great Britain by
CPI Cox & Wyman, Reading, RG1 8EX

To Suzy and John
and Jack and Brendan

Acknowledgments

Our great thanks to these top professionals who shared with us their valuable time and expertise during the writing of this book: Philip R. Hoffman, Dr. Humphrey Germaniuk, Captain Richard Conklin, Mickey Sherman, Clint Van Zandt, Dr. Maria Paige, Dr. Mike Sciarra, Darcy Hammerman Dalton, Michael Burke, and Stephen Donini.

Our special thanks to our stupendous researchers: Lynn Colomello, Lauren Sheftell, Ellie Shurtleff, and, of course, Mary Jordan, the woman with twelve pairs of hands.

WOMEN'S MURDER CLUB

Prologue

A THIEF IN THE NIGHT

One

SARAH WELLS STOOD on the roof of the carport and snaked her gloved hand through the hole she'd cut in the glass. Her pulse was thudding in her ears as she unlocked the double-hung window, opened the sash, and slid quietly into the darkened room. Once inside, she flattened herself against the wall and listened.

Voices rose from the floor below, and she heard the clanking of silverware against china. *Good timing,* Sarah thought. *In fact, perfect.*

But timing and execution were two different things entirely.

She switched on her miner's headlamp and took a 180-degree illuminated tour of the bedroom. She noted the console table to her left,

3

which was loaded with whatnots. She had to watch out for that table and the scatter rugs on the slick hardwood floors.

The lithe young woman quickly crossed the space, shut the door between the bedroom and hallway, and headed to the open closet, which smelled faintly of perfume. Leaving the door open just a crack, Sarah played her light over racks of clothing. She parted a curtain of long, beaded gowns, and there it was: a safe in the closet wall.

Sarah had bet on this. If Casey Dowling was like most socialites, she dressed for her dinner parties and wore her jewels. Chances were that she'd left her safe unlocked so she could put her jewels away later without having to punch in the combination again. Sarah tugged lightly on the safe's handle—and the heavy door swung open.

It was a go.

But she had to work fast. Three minutes, no more.

Sarah's headlamp lit up the contents of the safe while leaving her hands free to frisk the jumble of satin envelopes and silk-covered boxes. Way in the back was a brocaded box the size of a small loaf of bread. She undid the latch and lifted the lid on the mother lode.

Sarah gasped.

She'd read stories about Casey Dowling for two months and seen dozens of photos of her at society events, glittering with jewels. But she hadn't expected the sheer weight of diamonds and precious stones, the gleaming mounds of baroque pearls.

It was cra-zzzy. Casey Dowling owned all of this.

Well, not for long.

Sarah plucked bracelets and earrings and rings out of the box and stowed them in one of her two small duffel bags, the straps of which crisscrossed her chest. She paused to study a particular ring in its own leather case, to marvel at the frickin' wonder of it—when lights flashed on in the bedroom only yards from where she stood in the closet.

Sarah snapped off her light and dropped to a crouch, her heart rate shooting into overdrive as she heard the living, booming voice of Marcus Dowling, superstar actor of theater and the silver screen, bickering with his wife as he came into the room.

Sarah tucked all five feet eight of herself into a ball behind gowns and garment bags.

God, she was stupid.

While she'd been ogling the jewels, the Dowlings' dinner party had ended, and now she was going to get caught and be imprisoned for grand larceny. Her. A high school English teacher. It would be a scandal — and that was the least of it.

Sweat broke out under Sarah's knit cap. Drops of it rolled from her underarms down the sides of her black turtleneck as she waited for the Dowlings to switch on the closet light and find her squatting there, a thief in the night.

Two

CASEY DOWLING WAS trying to squeeze an admission from her husband, but Marcus wasn't having it.

"What the hell, Casey?" he snapped. "I wasn't staring at Sheila's boobs, for Christ's sake. Every single time we get together with people, you complain that I'm leering, and frankly, sweetheart, I find your paranoia very unattractive."

"Ohhhh no, Marcus. You? Leer at another woman? I'm soooo ashamed of myself for even having had the thought." Casey had a lovely laugh, even when it was colored with sarcasm.

"Silly cow," Marcus Dowling muttered.

Sarah imagined his handsome face, the thick gray hair falling across his brow as he scowled.

She imagined Casey, too — her willowy shape, her white-blond hair falling in a silvery sheet to her shoulder blades.

Casey cooed, "There, there. I've hurt your feelings."

"Forget it, love. I'm not in the mood now."

"Oh. Sorry. My mistake."

Sarah felt the rebuff as if it had happened to her. Then Marcus said, "Oh, for pity's sake. Don't cry. Come here."

The room went quiet for a few minutes, until Sarah heard a *whoosh* of bodies falling into plumped bedding, then murmuring — words she couldn't make out. Then the headboard began to tap against the wall, and Sarah thought, *Oh dear God, they're doing it.*

Images came to her of Marcus Dowling in *Susan and James* with Jennifer Lowe and in *Redboy* with Kimberly Kerry. She thought of Casey in Marcus's arms, her long legs wrapped around him. The tapping became more rhythmic and the moaning became louder and then there was a long, groaning exhalation from Marcus, and then — mercifully — it was over.

Someone used the bathroom after that, and *finally* the room went black.

Sarah squatted quietly behind the curtain of gowns for at least twenty minutes, and when the breathing outside the closet settled into sputters and snores, she opened the door and crawled to the window.

She was almost home free—but not there yet.

Sarah was quick and quiet as she vaulted to the windowsill, but when one leg followed the other, she hit the side of the console table—and it all went wrong.

There was the tinkling of sliding whatnots as the table tipped and then crashed, sending its load of picture frames and perfume bottles to the floor.

Holy crap.

Sarah froze, mind and body, as Casey Dowling bolted into a sitting position and yelled, "Who's there?"

Sarah's stark fear propelled her out the window. She hung on to the roof of the carport with all the strength in her fingertips, then released her grip and made the ten-foot drop.

She landed on grass, knees bent, no pain. And

as the Dowlings' bedroom light came on over-head, Sarah ran. She ripped off her headlamp and stuffed it into one of the duffels as she sprinted through the upscale San Francisco neighborhood of Nob Hill.

A few minutes later Sarah found her old Saturn where she'd left it in the parking lot outside a drugstore. She got into the car, closed the door, and locked it, as if that could keep out her fear. She started up the engine and released the hand brake, still panting, trying not to throw up as she drove toward home.

When she hit the straightaway of Pine Street, Sarah pulled off her cap and gloves, wiped her brow with the back of her hand, and thought hard about her escape from the Dowlings' bedroom.

She'd left nothing: no tools, no prints, no DNA. No nothing.

For now, at least, she was safe.

Honestly. She didn't know whether to laugh or to cry.

Three

CASEY'S EYES FLEW open in the dark.

Something had crashed. The table by the window! She felt a breeze on her face. The window was open. They never opened that window.

Someone was inside the house.

Casey sat up. "Who's there?" She clutched the blankets to her chin and screamed, "Marc! Someone is in the room."

Her husband groaned, "You're dreaming. Go back to sleep."

"Wake up! Someone is *here*," she hissed.

Casey fumbled with the table lamp, knocked her glasses onto the floor, found the switch, and turned on the light. *There.* The console table was turned over, everything broken, curtains blowing in the breeze.

"Do something, Marc. *Do* something."

Marcus Dowling worked out every day. He could still bench-press two hundred pounds, and he knew how to use a gun. He told his wife to be quiet, then opened his nightstand drawer and removed the .44 he kept fully loaded in a soft leather bag. He shucked the sack and gripped the gun.

Casey grabbed the bedside phone and pressed the numbers 9-1-1 with a shaking hand. She misdialed, then tried again as Marc, still half drunk, bellowed, *"Who's there?"* Even when he was serious, he sounded scripted. *"Show yourself."*

Marcus looked in the bathroom and the hallway, then said, "There's no one here, Casey. Just what I said."

Casey dropped the phone back into its cradle, shoved at the bedcovers, and went to the closet for her robe—and screamed.

"What is it now?"

White-faced, naked, Casey turned to her husband and said, "Oh my God, Marc, my jewelry is *gone*. The safe is almost *empty*."

A look came over Marc's face that was hard for Casey to read. It was as if he'd had an idea, and the idea was catching fire. Did he know who robbed them?

"Marc? What is it? What are you thinking?"

"Ah, I was thinking, *You can't take it with you*."

"What kind of bullshit is that? What do you mean?"

Dowling extended his right arm and aimed the gun at a mole between his wife's breasts. He pulled the trigger. *Boom*.

"*That's* what I mean," he said.

Casey Dowling opened her mouth, sucked in air, and exhaled as she looked down at her chest, at the blood pumping and bubbling out of the wound. She clasped her hands to her chest. She looked at her husband and gasped, "Help me."

He shot her again.

Then her knees buckled and she went down.

WOMEN'S MURDER CLUB

Part One

SNEAKY PETE

Chapter 1

PETER GORDON FOLLOWED the young mom out of Macy's and into the street outside the Stonestown Galleria. Mom was about thirty, her brown hair in a messy ponytail, wearing a lot of red: not just shorts but red sneakers and a red purse. Shopping bags hung from the handles of her baby's stroller.

Pete was behind the woman when she crossed Winston Drive, still almost on her heels as she entered the parking garage, talking to the infant as if he could understand her, asking him if he remembered where Mommy parked the car and what Daddy was making for dinner, chattering away, the whole running baby-talk commentary like a fuse lit by the woman's mouth, terminating at the charge inside Petey's brain.

But Petey stayed focused on his target. He listened and watched, kept his head down, hands in his pockets, and saw the woman unlock the hatch of her RAV4 and jam her shopping bags inside. He was only yards away from her when she hoisted the baby out of the stroller and folded the carriage into the back, too.

The woman was strapping the boy into the car seat when Pete started toward her.

"Ma'am? Can you help me out, please?"

The woman drew her brows together. *What do you want?* was written all over her face as she saw him. She got into the front seat now, keys in hand.

"Yes?" she said.

Pete Gordon knew that he looked healthy and clean and wide-eyed and trustworthy. His all-American good looks were an asset, but he wasn't vain. No more than a Venus flytrap was vain.

"I've got a flat," Pete said, throwing up his hands. "I really hate to ask, but could I use your cell phone to call Triple-A?"

He flashed a smile and got the dimples going, and at last she smiled, too, and said, "I do that—forget to charge the darned thing."

She dug into her purse, then looked up with the cell phone in hand. Her smile wavered as she read Pete's new expression, no longer eager to please but hard and determined.

She dropped her eyes to the gun he was holding—thinking that somehow she'd gotten it wrong—looked back into his face, and saw the chill in his dark eyes.

She jerked away from him, dropping her keys and her phone into the foot well. She climbed halfway into the backseat.

"Oh my God," she said. "Don't—do anything. I've got cash—"

Pete fired, the round whizzing through the suppressor, hitting the woman in the neck. She grabbed at the wound, blood spouting through her fingers.

"*My baby,*" she gasped.

"Don't worry. He won't feel anything. I promise," Pete Gordon said.

He shot the woman again, *poof,* this time in the side of her chest, then opened the back door and looked at the bawler, nodding off, mouth sticky with cotton candy, blue veins tracing a road map across his temple.

Chapter 2

A CAR SCREAMED down the ramp and squealed around the corner, speeding past Pete as he turned his face toward the concrete center island. He was sure he hadn't been seen, and anyway he'd done everything right. Strictly by the book.

The woman's open bag was lying inside the car. With his hand in his jacket pocket, using it as a kind of glove, he dug around in her junk, looking for her lipstick.

He found it, then swiveled up the bright-red tube.

He waited as a couple of gabby women in an Escalade drove up the ramp looking for a spot, then he took the lipstick tube between his thumb and forefinger and considered what he would write on the windshield.

He thought of writing FOR KENNY but changed his mind. He laughed to himself as he also considered and rejected PETEY WAS HERE.

Then he got real.

He printed WCF in bold red letters, four inches high, and underscored the writing with a smeary red line. Then he closed the lipstick and dropped it into his pocket, where it clicked against his gun.

Satisfied, he backed out of the car, shut the doors, wiped down the handles with the soft flannel lining of his baseball jacket, and walked to the elevator bank. He stood aside as the door opened and an old man wheeled his wife out onto the main floor of the garage. He kept his head down, avoiding eye contact with the old couple, and they ignored him.

That was good, but he wished he could tell them.

It was for Kenny. And it was by the book.

Pete Gordon got into the elevator and rode it up to the third floor, thinking he was having a really good day, the first good one in about a year.

It had been a long time coming, but he'd finally launched his master plan.

He was exhilarated, because he was absolutely sure it would work.

WCF, people. WCF.

Chapter 3

PETE GORDON DROVE down the looping ramp of the garage. He passed the dead woman's car on the ground floor but didn't even brake, confident that there was no blood outside the car, nothing to show that he'd been there.

With the garage as packed as it was, it could be hours before the mom and her bawler were found in that tidy spot near the end of the row.

Pete took it nice and slow, easing the car out of the garage and accelerating onto Winston, heading toward 19th Avenue. He reviewed the shooting in his mind as he waited at the light, thinking about how easy it had been—no wasted rounds, nothing forgotten—and how crazed it was going to make the cops.

Nothing worse than a motiveless crime, huh, Kenny?

The cops were going to bust their stones on this one, all right, and by the time they figured it out, he'd be living in another country and this crime would be one of the cold cases some old Homicide dick would never solve.

Pete took the long way home, up Sloat Boulevard, up and over Portola Drive, where he waited for the Muni train to pass with commuters all in a row, and finally up Clipper Street toward his crappy apartment in the Mission.

It was almost dinnertime, and his own little bawlers would be puffing up their cheeks, getting ready to sound the alarm. He had his key out when he got to the apartment. He opened the lock and gave the door a kick.

He could smell the baby's diapers from the doorway, the little stinker standing in the kiddie cage in the middle of the floor, hanging on to the handrail, crying out as soon as he saw his dad.

"Daddy!" Sherry called. "He needs to be changed."

"Goody," Peter Gordon said. "Shut up, stink

bomb," he told the boy. "I'll get to you in a minute." He took the remote control from his daughter's hand, switched from the cartoons, and checked the news.

The stock market was down. Oil prices were up. He watched the latest Hollywood update. Nothing was said about two bodies found in the Stonestown Galleria parking lot.

"I'm hungry," Sherry said.

"Well, which is it first? Dinner or poop?"

"Poop first," she said.

"All right, then."

Pete Gordon picked up the baby, as dear to him as a sack of cement, not even sure the little shit was his, although even if he was, he still didn't care. He put the baby on its back on the changing table and went through the ritual, holding the kiddo by the ankles, wiping him down, dusting his butt with powder, wrapping him up in Pampers, then putting him back in the kiddie cage.

"Franks and beans?" he asked his daughter.

"My absolute favorite," Sherry said, putting a pigtail in her mouth.

"Put a shirt on the stink bomb," Pete Gordon

said, "so your mother doesn't have a gas attack when she gets home."

Gordon microwaved some formula for the stink bomb and opened the canned franks and beans. He turned on the undercabinet TV and the stove, what wifey should be doing instead of him, the bitch, and dumped the contents of the can into a pot.

The beans were burning when the breaking news came on.

Huh. Look at that, Pete thought.

Some dork from ABC was holding a microphone, standing in front of Borders. College kids mugged behind him as he said, "We have learned that there has been a shooting at the Stonestown garage. Sources report a gruesome double homicide that you will not believe. We'll keep you posted as details are released. Back to you, Yolanda."

Chapter 4

YUKI CASTELLANO STEPPED out of her office and called down the line of cubicles to Nicky Gaines, "You ready, Wonder Boy? Or do you want to meet me downstairs?"

"I'm coming," Gaines said. "Who said I wasn't coming?"

"How do I look?" she asked him, already moving toward the elevator that would take them from the DA's office to the courtroom.

"You look fierce, Batwoman. Miss Hot Multicultural USA."

"Shut up." She laughed at her protégé. "Just be ready to prompt me if I blank, God forbid."

"You're not going to blank. You're going to send Jo-Jo to the big house."

"Ya think?"

"I *know*. Don't you?"

"Uh-huh. I just have to make sure the jury knows it, too."

Nicky stabbed the elevator button, and Yuki went back to her thoughts. In about twenty minutes, she was going to make her closing argument in the state's case against Adam "Jo-Jo" Johnson.

Since she'd been with the DA's office, she'd taken on more than a few crappy cases that the DA was determined to try: she'd work eighteen-hour days, earning "atta girls" from her boss, Leonard "Red Dog" Parisi, and score points with the jury, all of which would give her high expectations.

And then she'd lose.

Yuki was becoming famous for losing — and that stank because she was a fighter and a winner. And she just frickin' hated to lose. But she never *thought* she'd lose — and this time was no different.

Her case was solid. She'd laid it out like a hand of solitaire. The jury had an easy job. The defendant wasn't just guilty, he was guilty as *sin*.

Nicky held open the studded leather door to

the courtroom, and Yuki walked smartly down the center aisle of the oak-paneled chamber. She noticed that the gallery was filling up with spectators, mostly press and law students. And as she approached the prosecution table, she saw that Jo-Jo Johnson and his attorney, Jeff Asher, were in their seats.

The stage was set.

She nodded to her opponent and noted the defendant's appearance. Jo-Jo's hair was combed and he was wearing a nice suit, but he looked dazed as only a mope who'd fried his brain on drugs could look. She hoped that very soon he would look worse, once she nailed him on manslaughter in the first degree.

"Jo-Jo looks like he's been smoking ganja," Nicky murmured to Yuki as he pulled out her chair.

"Or else he believes his lawyer's bull," Yuki said loud enough for her opponent to hear. "Jo-Jo may think he's going to walk, but he'll be busing it to Pelican Bay."

Asher looked at her and smirked, showing Yuki with his body language that he thought he was going to whip her.

It was an act.

Yuki hadn't gone up against Asher before, but after less than a year in the public defender's office, Asher had gotten a reputation as a "bomb" —a killer attorney who blew up the prosecution's case and got his client off. Asher was formidable because he had it all: charisma, boyish good looks, and a Harvard Law degree. And he had his father, a top-notch litigator who was coaching his son from the sidelines.

But none of that mattered today.

The evidence, the witnesses, and the confession were all on her side. Jo-Jo Johnson was hers.

Chapter 5

JUDGE STEVEN RABINOWITZ took a last look at the pictures of his new condo in Aspen, then turned off his iPhone, cracked his knuckles, and said, "Are the People ready, Ms. Castellano?"

"We are, Your Honor," said Yuki.

She stood, her glossy black hair with the new silver streak in front falling forward as she straightened the hem of her suit jacket. Then she stepped quickly to the lectern in the center of the well.

She turned her eyes toward the jury box and gave the jurors a smile. A couple of them smiled back, but for the most part they were expressionless. She couldn't read them at all.

But that was okay.

She just had to give the greatest closing of her life, as if the dead scumbag victim were the best and brightest of men, and as if this were the last case she would ever try.

"Ladies and Gentlemen," she said, "Dr. Lincoln Harris is dead because this man, Adam J. Johnson, knew Dr. Harris was in mortal danger and let him die with willful disregard for his life. In California, that's manslaughter in the first degree.

"We know what happened on the night of March fourteenth because, after waiving his right to remain silent, after waiving his right to counsel, Mr. Johnson told the police how and why he let Dr. Harris expire when he could have easily saved his life."

Yuki let her words resonate in the chamber, shuffling her cards on the lectern before continuing her closing argument.

"On the evening in question, the defendant, who had been employed by Dr. Harris as a handyman, went out to get cocaine for the doctor and himself.

"He returned within the hour, and the defendant and the plaintiff ingested this cocaine.

Shortly after that, Dr. Harris OD'd. How do we know that?

"The defendant told the police—and it was borne out by medical experts—that it was clear Dr. Harris was *in extremis*. He was foaming at the mouth and eventually lost consciousness. But, rather than call an ambulance, the defendant used this opportunity to remove a thousand dollars and an ATM card from Dr. Harris's wallet.

"Mr. Johnson then used Dr. Harris's ATM card, took another thousand dollars, and bought himself a new leather jacket and a pair of boots at Rochester Big & Tall.

"After that," Yuki told them, "the defendant bought more cocaine and hired a prostitute, Elizabeth Wu, whom he brought back to Dr. Harris's home.

"Over the next several hours, Ms. Wu and Mr. Johnson snorted coke, had sex a few times, and at one point, according to Mr. Johnson's statement, discussed how to dispose of Dr. Harris's body once he died. That, Ladies and Gentlemen, shows 'consciousness of guilt.'

"Adam Johnson absolutely knew that the doctor was dying. But he didn't call for help for fifteen hours," Yuki said, slapping the lectern. "Fifteen hours. Finally, at the behest of Ms. Wu, Mr. Johnson finally called nine one one, but it was too little, too late. Dr. Harris died in the ambulance en route to the hospital.

"Now, we all know that the defense has no defense.

"When facts are against them, defense lawyers resort to theatrics and to blaming the victim.

"Mr. Asher has told you that Dr. Harris lost his license to practice medicine because he used drugs. And that he cheated on his wife. That's true, and *so what?* The victim wasn't a saint, but even imperfect people have a right to humane treatment. And they have a right to justice.

"The defense has portrayed Adam Johnson as a hapless gofer who didn't know an OD from a CD.

"That's fiction. Adam Johnson knew what he was doing. He's admitted to all of it: the willful disregard as well as the fun he had that night, stealing and shopping and snorting coke and having sex while Dr. Harris lay dying.

"That's why there can be only one verdict. The People ask you to find Adam Johnson guilty on three counts: of grand larceny, of intent to deal narcotics, and of reckless disregard for the life of a human being—that is, manslaughter in the first degree."

Chapter 6

YUKI HUDDLED WITH Gaines in the hallway outside the courtroom during the ten-minute recess.

"You knocked their socks off," Gaines told her.

Yuki nodded. She combed her mind for mistakes and didn't find any. She hadn't blanked, hadn't sputtered or blown her lines, hadn't come off as rehearsed. She had no regrets. She only wished her mom could have been here to see her.

She said to her number two, "Jo-Jo did it. He said he did it, and we proved it." Yuki's heart was still pumping adrenaline, the good kind. A bit like champagne.

Nicky nudged her, and Yuki looked up. She saw that the bailiff had opened the leather-paneled door. The pair re-entered the courtroom and took their seats. Yuki's mouth went suddenly dry as the court was called into session.

And now the fear factor started nibbling at her confidence. Asher would have the last word. Could he convince the jury to let Johnson off? She thought ahead to the worst possible result— a finding in favor of the defendant. After that, Asher's dad would give his son a party at the Ruby Skye, and she would slink home alone.

The humiliation would be all hers.

Beside her, Nicky doodled a caricature of her with a star on her chest and a halo behind her head. She managed a smile, and then the room fell silent.

Judge Rabinowitz asked Asher if the defense was ready to close, and he answered, "Yes, Your Honor, we are."

Like a Thoroughbred into the starting gate, Asher nearly pranced toward the jury box. He put his hand on the railing and—while standing no more than a yard away from the jurors in the front row, close enough for the foreperson to see the comb marks in his hair and the sparkle on his dental veneers—began his summation.

"Folks, I don't have any notes because Adam Johnson's defense is as simple and as clear as day.

"He's not a doctor. He doesn't know anything about sick people or about medicine. He didn't know that Dr. Harris was in serious distress.

"Adam Johnson is a handyman.

"Lincoln Harris was a doctor of medicine.

"And, as the medical examiner told you, Lincoln Harris didn't die from cocaine overdose. He died from cocaine and a self-injected dose of heroin.

"What happened is that those drugs interacted, and that proved fatal. Dr. Harris knew what drugs did to the body, and he took them anyway. For all anyone knows, he intended to die.

"I think Mr. Johnson would agree that if he had it to do again, when he saw that Dr. Harris was ill, he would have immediately called nine one one. He probably would have done everything different that night, but he made some mistakes.

"Yes, he's guilty of stealing two thousand dollars from a rich boss who had given him his ATM pin number.

"Yes, he's guilty of giving those drugs to Ms. Wu, a known drug user and a prostitute, and while this is true, it's a technicality. He wasn't actually dealing. He used drugs for recreation.

"As for consciousness of guilt, I submit to you folks that my client was just shooting the bull with Ms. Wu when they discussed 'dumping the body.'

"They didn't do it, did they?" Asher asked rhetorically. "Mr. Johnson called for an ambulance. The facts are clear. My client didn't know if Dr. Harris was dying or if he was going to wake up with a bad headache. He's no genius, but he's not a bad guy.

"And so we ask you to find him 'not guilty' of manslaughter, because he simply *did not do it*."

Chapter 7

I LEFT THE Homicide squad room in a hurry that evening, determined to get out of Jacobi's line of sight before I got drafted into someone else's case. I'd just stepped into the elevator when, damn it, my cell phone buzzed.

It was Yuki; she was funny, passionate, and going through a rough time, so I pressed the phone to my ear and she peppered me with her customary rat-a-tat speech.

"Lindsay, my head's spinning off my neck. Can you meet me at MacBain's? Like, now?"

"What's wrong?"

"You're busy."

"I've got plans," I said, "but I can have a quick beer—"

"I'll meet you in five."

MacBain's Beers O' the World Pub is a cops-and-lawyers hangout two blocks from the Hall of Justice. I got my car out of the all-day lot and headed east on Bryant, telling myself that I'd still have time to pick up the shrimp on the way home.

I entered the bar, found a tiny table near the window, and had just ordered two Coronas from the waitress when I saw Yuki elbowing her way through the crowd, coming toward me. She was talking before she sat down.

"You ordered? Good. How are you? Okay?"

The waitress brought the beer, and Yuki asked for a burger well-done with cheese fries.

"You're not eating?" she said.

"I'm cooking a late dinner for Joe."

"Ah."

She put a hand to her brow as if shielding her eyes from the light bouncing off my engagement ring.

"Must be nice."

"Yeah," I said, grinning at her.

Being engaged was still new to me after months and months of a cross-country roller-coaster romance. Now Joe and I lived together, and we still hadn't sat down to dinner at the same time in two weeks. I'd promised him shrimp pomodoro tonight, and I was looking forward to the whole deal: the cooking, the supping, the afterglow. "So what's going on?" I asked Yuki.

She drained half her glass before answering. "My victim isn't just scum, he's dead scum, and Jo-Jo is cute and stupid. The women jurists looked at him, Linds, like they wanted to breast-feed him."

I'd stopped by the courtroom to watch Yuki's closing argument, and I had to agree. Dr. Lincoln Harris was dead slime, and while Jo-Jo Johnson was hardly better — he was alive. And he looked like a man without a clue.

"Asher could actually win," Yuki wailed. "I quit private practice for *this*? Help me, Linds. Should I find a good-paying job in a corporate law firm?"

My phone vibrated on my hip again. I looked down at the caller ID. Jacobi. My ex-partner and current boss, whose gut reaction to everything is to call me. Old habits die hard. I keyed the button and said, "Boxer," into the mouthpiece.

"There's been a double homicide, Lindsay. It's got 'psycho' written all over it."

"Did you call Paul Chi? He's back from vacation. I'll bet he's home right now."

"I want you on this," Jacobi growled.

After more than ten years of working together, we were almost able to read each other's mind. Jacobi sounded freaked out, like someone had walked over his grave.

"What's this about, Warren?" I asked him, already knowing my best-laid plans for the evening were shot.

"One of the vics is a young kid," Jacobi said.

He gave me the address—the parking garage near the galleria. "Conklin just left. He'll be there in a couple of minutes."

"I'm on my way," I told him.

Chapter 8

I CLOSED MY phone and promised Yuki a longer, better talk about her career after the jury came back. I said, "Your closing was outstanding, girlfriend. Don't quit." I kissed her cheek and fled the bar.

I drove my Explorer toward Market and got gridlocked. I put the Kojak light on my roof and hit the siren. Vehicles parted reluctantly, and I finally reached the entrance to the garage near the Stonestown Galleria.

The mouth of the garage was cordoned off and blocked by a grumbling crowd of car owners. I held up my shield, ducked under the tape, and signed the log. Officer Joe Sorbero looked gray, as if he'd never seen death before.

"You're the first officer on the scene?"

"Yes, ma'am."

"You okay, Joe?"

"I've been better, Sergeant," he said, smiling weakly. "I've got kids, you know." He pointed out a blue RAV4 parked toward the far end of the row. "Your next nightmare is right over there."

I followed Sorbero's finger and saw Inspector Rich Conklin standing between a couple of vehicles at the end of the aisle, peering into the driver's-side window of the RAV4.

When Jacobi moved up to lieutenant, Conklin became my partner. He's smart and disturbingly handsome, and he's got the makings of a first-class detective. It wouldn't shock anyone if he made captain one day, but right now he reports to me.

He came toward me before I could reach the scene.

"Brace yourself, Linds."

"Fill me in."

"White female, about thirty, name of Barbara Ann Benton. The other victim is an infant. Might be a year old. Both were shot point-blank. The ME and CSU are on the way."

"Who called it in?"

"A lady who was parked in the spot next to the RAV4. I interviewed her and sent her home. She didn't see anything. So far, no one did. Unis are going through the trash cans, and we've collected the surveillance tape."

"Are you thinking the baby was collateral damage?"

"No way," Conklin said. "He was capped on purpose."

I approached the SUV and sucked in my breath as I looked inside. Barbara Ann Benton was slumped awkwardly in the front seat, half facing the rear as if she'd tried to climb over the divide.

I saw two obvious gunshot wounds: one to the neck and another to the side of her chest. Then I forced myself to look past the mom to the child in his car seat.

The baby boy had a glaze of pink candy on his lips and on the fingers of his right hand. The rear window was spattered with blood. The child had been shot through the temple at close range.

Conklin was right.

The baby's death was no accident. In fact, the

shot was so precise, the kid could have been the prime target.

I hoped that the little boy hadn't realized what was happening.

I hoped he hadn't had time to be afraid.

Chapter 9

"WHAT DO YOU make of this, Linds?"

Conklin called to my attention the vivid red letters printed on the windshield. I stared, riveted by the sight. This is what Jacobi had been talking about when he'd said that the crime scene had "'psycho' written all over it."

He hadn't said it was written in lipstick.

The letters "WCF" meant nothing to me, except the fact that only wacko killers deliberately leave a signature. It reminded me of cases I'd caught where the killer had signed his crimes. And it brought back the bad old days when the Backstreet Killer had terrified San Francisco in the '90s, a murderer who took eight innocent lives, left signatures and notes for the police, and was never caught. A chill went down the back of my neck.

"Those shopping bags in the rear," I said to Conklin. "Were they looted?" I was hoping.

My partner shook his head no and said, "Looks like a hundred bucks in the victim's wallet. This wasn't a robbery. This was an execution. Two of them."

Questions were flooding my mind. Why hadn't gunshots been reported? Why had the killer targeted these people? Was it random or personal? Why had he killed a child?

I turned toward the sound of an engine's roar and saw the coroner's van heading toward us, tires screeching as it braked twenty feet away.

Dr. Claire Washburn got out of the van wearing blue scrubs and a Windbreaker—black with white letters spelling out MEDICAL EXAMINER front and back. Despite the odds of a black woman succeeding in her profession when she first got started, Claire had done it. In my opinion, she's the finest forensic pathologist west of the Rockies. She's also the friend of my heart, and although we work three flights and eighty feet away in adjoining buildings,

I hadn't seen her in more than a week.

"Jesus God, what is *this?*" she asked as she hugged me and took in the scene over my shoulder.

I walked Claire toward the RAV4 and stood next to her as she looked into the car and saw the dead woman in a crouch, half facing her baby.

Claire jerked back as she took in the sight of the dead child, her face reflecting the same horror the rest of us were feeling, maybe more. "That baby is the same age as my Ruby," she said. "Who kills a baby too young to tell what happened?"

"Maybe it's payback for something. Drug deal. Gambling debt. Or maybe the husband did it."

I was thinking, *Please let it be something like that.*

Claire took her Minolta out of her kit and fired off two shots of Barbara Ann Benton from where we stood, then went around to the other side of the vehicle and took two more.

When she started shooting pictures of the baby, I saw the tears in her eyes. She wiped them with the back of her hand. I couldn't remember the last time I'd seen Claire cry.

"Mom let the killer get this close," Claire said.

"Gunpowder stippling is on her cheek and neck. She tried to shield her baby with her body, and still the bastard shot the child in the head. And here's something new: I don't recognize this stippling pattern."

"What does that mean?"

"Means WCF has some rare kind of gun."

Chapter 10

THE BENTONS' HOUSE was a modest two-bedroom on 14th Avenue, blue with white trim, spray-on Fourth of July decorations still on the picture window and a pull toy on the steps. Conklin rang the bell, and when Richard Benton opened the front door, I knew that we were seeing the last happy moment of the man's life.

When a married woman is killed, her husband is involved more than half the time, but I found Richard Benton believably devastated when we told him the shocking news—and he had an alibi. He'd been home with his five-year-old when the shooting took place, had roasted a chicken for dinner, and had sent a constant stream of e-mail to his office during that time.

Benton was at first disbelieving and then shattered, but Conklin and I talked to him anyway, about his marriage, about Barbara's friends and coworkers, and asked if there'd been any threats against her. He said, "Barbara is nothing but love. I don't know what we're going to do..." And then he broke down again.

I checked in with Jacobi at nine. I told him that until I ran Richard Benton's name through NCIC, he was in the clear, and that Benton didn't know the initials "WCF."

"Barbara was a nurse's aide," I told Jacobi. "Worked at a nursing home. We'll interview the others on her shift first thing in the morning."

"I'm going to hand that job off to Samuels and Lemke," Jacobi said. He had a strangled sound in his voice for the second time in as many hours.

"Hand it off? Excuse me? What's that about?"

"Something new just came in, Boxer."

Honest to God, I was running out of gas, going into my thirteenth straight hour on the job. Behind me, in a room shimmering with anguish, Conklin was telling Richard Benton to come to the ME's office to identify the victims.

"Something new on the Benton case?" I asked

Jacobi. Maybe the husband had a record for domestic violence. Maybe a witness had come forward, or perhaps CSI had found something inside the RAV4.

Jacobi said, "No, this just happened. If you want me to give it to Chi and McNeil, I will. But you and Conklin are going to want in."

"Don't be too sure, Jacobi."

"You've heard of Marcus Dowling?"

"The actor?"

"His wife was just shot by an intruder," Jacobi told me. "I'm on my way over to the Dowling house now."

Chapter 11

THE DOWLING HOUSE is on Nob Hill, a sprawling mansion taking up most of the block, ivy growing up the walls, potted topiaries on either side of the large oak door. It couldn't have been more different from the Bentons' humble home.

Before Conklin could reach for the bell, Jacobi opened the door. His face was sagging from stress. His eyelids drooped, and he almost looked older tonight than he had when we'd both taken bullets on Larkin Street.

"It happened in the bedroom," he told me and my partner. "Second floor. After you've taken a look at the scene, join us downstairs. I'll be in the library with Dowling."

The bedroom shared by Marcus and Casey Dowling looked like it had been ripped from the pages of a Neiman Marcus catalog.

The bed, centered on the west-facing wall, was the size of Catalina, with a button-tucked bronze silk headboard, silk throw pillows, and rumpled satin bedding in bronze and gold. There were more tassels in this room than backstage at the Mitchell Brothers' *Girls, Girls, Girls!!!* review.

A dainty console table was on the floor, surrounded by broken knickknacks. Taffeta curtains swelled at the open window, but I could still smell the undertones of gunpowder in the air.

Charlie Clapper, director of our Crime Scene Unit, was taking pictures of Casey Dowling's body. He flapped his hand toward me and Conklin in greeting and said, "Frickin' shame, a beautiful woman like this." He stepped back so we could take a look.

Casey Dowling was naked, lying faceup on the floor, her platinum hair splayed around her, blood on her palms. It made me think she'd clasped her hands to the chest wound before she fell.

"Her husband says he was downstairs rinsing dinner dishes when he heard two gunshots," Clapper told me. "When he came into the room, his wife was lying here. That table and the bric-a-brac were broken on the floor, and the window was open."

"Was anything taken?" Conklin asked.

"There's some jewelry missing from the safe in the closet. Dowling says the contents were insured for a couple of million."

Clapper walked to the window and held back the curtain, revealing a hole cut in the glass.

"Intruder used a glass cutter, then opened the lock. Drawers look untouched. The safe wasn't blown, so either he knew the combination or, more likely, the safe was already open. Bullets are inside the missus. No shell casings. This was a neat job until he knocked over the table on the way out. We've just gotten started. Maybe we'll get lucky and find prints or trace."

Clapper is a pro, with some twenty-five years on the force, a good part of it in Homicide before he went over to crime scene investigation. He's sharp, and he actually helps without getting in the way.

I said, "So this was a burglary that went to hell?"

Clapper shrugged. "Like all professional cat burglars, this one was organized, even fastidious. Maybe he carries a gun for emergencies, but packing goes against the type."

"So what happened?" I wondered out loud. "The husband wasn't in the room. The victim wasn't armed—she wasn't even *dressed*. What made a cat burglar fire on a naked woman?"

Chapter 12

CONKLIN AND I took the curving staircase down to the main floor. I found the library by following the familiar, resonant, English-accented voice of Marcus Dowling.

I'd seen all of his older films, the ones where he'd played a spy or was a romantic lead, and even some of his more recent films, where he'd played a heavy. I'd always liked him.

I stepped through the open door to the library, and Dowling was standing there barefoot, wearing blue trousers and an unbuttoned white shirt. I admit to feeling a little starstruck. Marcus Dowling, the next best thing to Sean Connery. He was telling Jacobi about the senseless murder of his wife when

Conklin and I came through the door.

Jacobi introduced us, telling Dowling that the three of us would be working the case together.

I shook hands with the film legend, then sat at the edge of a leather sofa. Dowling was clearly distraught. And I noticed something else. His hair was wet.

Dowling didn't sit down. He repeated his story as he paced around the book-lined room.

"Casey and I had the Devereaus over for dinner. François and his wife, Sheila — he's directing my new film."

"We'll need their contact numbers," I said.

"I'll give you all the numbers you want," he said, "but they had already left when this happened. Casey had gone upstairs to dress for bed. I was tidying up down here. I heard a loud bang coming from upstairs." His forehead rumpled. "It didn't even occur to me that it was a gunshot. I called out to Casey. She didn't answer."

"What happened next, Mr. Dowling?"

"I called her again, and then as I was heading upstairs, I heard another bang. This time I thought it was a gunshot, and right after that, I heard glass breaking.

"I was all emotional by this time, Inspectors. I don't know what happened after...after I saw my girl lying on the floor. I grabbed her in my arms," he said, his voice cracking.

"Her head fell back, and she wasn't breathing. I must have called the police. I saw my bloody handprint on the phone. Afterward, I realized that the safe was nearly empty.

"Whoever did this must have known Casey," Dowling continued, weeping now. "He must have known that she didn't always lock the safe, because dialing the combination was just...too bloody boring.

"Killing Casey was so insane," Dowling went on. He was rubbing his chest when he said to Jacobi, "Just tell me what I can do to help you catch the animal who did this."

I was about to ask Marcus Dowling why he'd showered while waiting for the police to arrive when Conklin got ahead of me, inquiring, "Mr. Dowling, do you own a gun?"

Dowling turned a wild-eyed stare on Conklin. His face went rigid with pain. He clutched his left arm and said, "Something's wrong."

Then he keeled over and dropped to the floor.

Chapter 13

JESUS CHRIST! MARCUS Dowling was dying.

Conklin found the aspirin, Jacobi cushioned Dowling's head with a throw pillow, and I called Dispatch. I repeated the house address and shouted, "Fifty-year-old male! Heart attack!"

Dowling was still writhing when the ambulance arrived, and the big man was loaded onto a gurney and carried out through the door. Jacobi rode with Dowling to the hospital, leaving me and Conklin to canvass the neighborhood.

Lights from fantastic neighboring homes punctuated the darkness along the tree-lined street. I was worried about this new case. Because Casey Dowling had been wealthy and famous, the public pressure to find her killer would squeeze the politicos, who would, in turn, squeeze us. The SFPD was already suffering from budget deficits and too little manpower. Add to that the public expectation that homicides could be solved in an hour between commercial breaks, and I knew we were in for a humongous, spotlighted nightmare.

I hoped Clapper would come up with a good lead in the lab, because right now, along with next to nothing to go on, I was getting a bad feeling that what Marcus had told us was all wrong.

"Why would a burglar shoot Casey Dowling?" I asked Conklin as we walked up the street.

"What Clapper said. The burglar carried a gun in case he ran into an emergency."

"Like a surprised homeowner?"

"Exactly."

"Casey Dowling wasn't armed."

"True. Maybe she recognized the intruder," Conklin said. "You know those stories Cindy's been doing on Hello Kitty?"

Cindy is Cindy Thomas, a crime reporter at the *San Francisco Chronicle* and a friend to the end with a great mind for solving whodunits.

Recently Cindy had been writing about a cat burglar who'd been doing second-story jobs, always breaking in when the homeowners were having dinner on the first floor and the alarm system was turned off. This burglar made off with only jewelry—which had not turned up. Cindy had dubbed the cat burglar "Hello Kitty," and it stuck.

Here's what was known about Hello Kitty: he was fit, deft, and fast, and had a huge pair of stones.

"Think about it," Conklin said. "Hello Kitty seems to know when these wealthy people are having dinner parties. What if he's part of the same social circle? If Casey Dowling recognized him, maybe shooting her was his only way out."

"Not a bad theory," I said to Conklin as we took the walk up to the front steps of the manse next door. "But wait a sec. What did you make of Dowling's wet hair?"

"He washed off his wife's blood."

"So he leaped into the shower after Casey was murdered," I said. "It seems weird to me."

"So what's your theory? Homicide One Oh One?"

"Why not? Because Dowling's a movie star? Something about him isn't right. He told Clapper he heard two gunshots. He told us he heard a noise, and then sometime after that, he heard a second sound, and that time he was sure it was a shot."

My partner said, "Could be he was just summing up, telling the story in shorthand."

"Could be shorthand," I said. "Or could be he's making up the story as he goes along and can't keep it straight."

Chapter 14

THE HOME NEXT to the Dowlings' was set back from the street and had a groundskeeper's house in the side yard and two deluxe cars in the driveway.

I pressed the bell, and chimes rang. The front door opened, and a brown-haired boy of about ten, wearing a rugby shirt over pajama bottoms, gazed up at us and asked who we were.

"I'm Sergeant Boxer. This is Inspector Conklin. Are your parents at home?"

"Kellll-yyyy!"

The boy turned out to be Evan Richards, and Kelly was his babysitter, a woman in her mid-twenties who had been watching *Project Runway* in the media room when she heard the sirens screaming up the street.

"Casey Dowling was killed?" she asked. "That's crazy. That burglar could have come here! Evan, can you grab the phone? I have to call your parents."

"I think I saw something," the boy said. "I was staring out my bedroom window, and someone ran past the house. Like, in the shadows under the trees."

"Could you describe him?" Conklin asked the boy.

Evan shook his head. "Just someone running. Wearing black. I heard him huffing as he ran."

I asked if this person was big or small, if there was anything special about the way he ran.

"I thought he was just a jogger, you know? He was wearing a cap, I think. I was looking down at the top of his head."

Conklin left his card with the boy's babysitter and asked Evan to please call if he remembered anything else. Then we headed down the block toward the next house.

I said to Conklin, "So maybe we have a live

witness to Kitty making a run for it." And then my cell phone rang.

Yuki, sending a text message: *Call me.*

I hit the recall button, and Yuki picked up.

"God! I know her!" Yuki said.

"Know who?"

"Casey Dowling."

Frickin' grapevine. How could she have heard already?

"We went to law school together, Lindsay. Damn it. Casey was a sweetheart. A doll. When you catch the shooter, I'm going to fight for the case, and then I'm going to send Casey Dowling's killer straight to hell."

Chapter 15

SARAH WELLS SHUT her bedroom door and locked it. She was still panting from her escapade, her hands still shaking. She stood in front of her mirror, fluffed up her hair, and looked at herself —hard.

Did it show?

Her skin was so white, it was almost transparent, and her brown eyes were huge. She thought about her husband telling her she could look good if she'd ever try, but when he told her that, she became even more determined to look exactly as she was: a twenty-eight-year-old schoolteacher with a second life. And she wasn't even talking about the burglaries.

Sarah put her two duffel bags down on the

floor, then opened the bottom drawer of the big, old American Waterfall dresser. Like her, the dresser held secrets.

Sarah took the piles of T-shirts and sweatpants out of the bottom drawer and pried up the drawer's false bottom. She held her breath, hoping, as always, that the jewelry was still there.

It was.

Each of her hauls had its own soft fabric bag, five collections of astonishing jewelry, and now the Dowling take made an even half dozen.

Sarah unzipped the bag with her latest haul and looked into the glorious tangle of jewels that had, until recently, belonged to a movie star's wife. It was the most unbelievable stuff: totally insane and wonderful sapphires and diamonds; rings and necklaces and bracelets; jewelry that could be worth hundreds of thousands of dollars or more.

She'd pulled off the burglary by the slimmest margin—a squeaker, for God's sake. She was safe for now, but she still had a big problem: how to get rid of the goods.

Maury Green, her mentor and fence, was dead, killed at the airport by a cop's bullet meant for his client, a jewel thief who'd been running from the police. Maury had been a good teacher and friend. It was truly depressing that he hadn't lived to celebrate her success and to collect his share.

Maury, like other good fences, paid out about 10 percent of the jewelry's retail value. It didn't seem like a lot, considering the hell that would rain down on her if she got caught, but still, it was a ton of money compared to what she earned as a teacher. And now Maury was gone.

The longer she held on to the jewelry, the greater her chance of getting caught with it. Sarah cupped a double handful of Casey Dowling's treasure and rocked her hands under a table lamp so that the light bounced off the facets.

Behind her locked bedroom door, Sarah Wells became mesmerized by the gorgeous refracting light.

Chapter 16

SARAH WELLS WASN'T the first cat burglar to do break-ins while dinner was on the table. She'd studied the greats, the Dinnertime Burglar and the Dinner Set Gang. Between them, they'd scored tens of millions in jewels using simple no-tech tools while their victims lingered over coffee and dessert on the floor below. Like her role models, Sarah thoroughly researched her intended targets and studied their movements. But with all the news about Hello Kitty, she marveled at how her victims felt so secure with the lights on that they didn't set their security alarms.

Their magical thinking was just *amazing*. And woo-hoo for that.

As Sarah gloried in the Dowlings' former riches, one special item reached out to her and hooked her in. It was a ring with a really large, pale-yellow stone, maybe twenty karats, cushion-cut and anchored in a thoroughly gaudy setting.

She took a rough count of the pavé jewels surrounding the center stone and tallied 120 little diamonds.

What a ring!

This thing was a frickin' gasper. It just shrieked romance. Marcus Dowling had undoubtedly given this ring to his wife for some special occasion, and now Sarah wondered what it could be worth.

She had learned a lot about precious stones since she'd started moonlighting as a cat burglar, but she wasn't a true gemologist and was really curious to know what she had.

She stashed the rest of the Dowling loot and her bag of tools into the bottom drawer of the dresser, put back the false lid, and piled her clothes on top of it. Then she shut the drawer and fished a pictorial guide to gemstones out from under the armoire, taking it with her into the double bed.

Paging through the book, she found a couple of matches to the stone. Possibly the ring was a topaz or a yellow tourmaline. No — there was a hint of green in Casey Dowling's big, yellow stone. Which probably made it a citrine, a flashy but not supervaluable stone. That was even more reason Sarah wanted to keep this ring.

While she knew that holding on to stolen merchandise could be a terrible mistake, she had to find a way to keep this one thing. She wanted more than a souvenir. She wanted a trophy. A reward. And now she was thinking that the thing to do was to have the yellow stone reset as a pendant.

She remembered something her grandmother had said to her mother, who had said it to her: "On some people, rhinestones look like diamonds. On others, diamonds look like rhinestones."

Sarah thought that, on her — with her T.J. Maxx wardrobe and plain looks — citrine would look like glass. She stood in front of the mirror and held the yellow stone to her black turtleneck, just under her collarbone.

It looked much smaller when it wasn't a ring.

She was sure that, once reset, this stone would

keep her secret. As Sarah stared at herself in the mirror, there was a loud knock on the door. It was her husband, Trevor.

"Why is the door locked, missy? What are you doing? Having fun with yourself?"

"You could say that," Sarah said.

"Let me in."

"No."

"Let me in!"

Sarah put the ring under the hollowed-out base of the lamp on her night table.

"Go to hell!" she shouted.

He was shaking the door, kicking at it. Sarah went over and unlocked it. *Just another day,* she thought as she let Trevor into the bedroom. *Just another day in the secret life of Sarah Wells.*

Chapter 17

SARAH SLAMMED THE front door of her apartment and marched out to the car thinking about frickin' Trevor, who had begged her, "Wait just another minute." Only it was an unbearable twenty minutes under his fat, nasty body, and now she was borderline late to work—again.

Sarah headed her Saturn onto Delores Street and got onto the freeway, making up lost time. She switched on the radio and found "*Good Morning* with Lisa Kerz and Rosemary Van Buren, *the* place for traffic, weather, and local news."

Lisa Kerz was saying, "Rosemary, this is the latest on Casey Dowling, who we've just learned was shot last night."

Shot. What was that? Sarah gripped the wheel.

"Do the police have a lead on who killed her?" Van Buren asked.

Killed her?

Sarah's heart thundered in her chest. What kind of lie was this? Casey Dowling was alive and screaming when she had escaped from the Dowling house.

Casey had been alive.

"No, this is about Marcus Dowling," said Kerz. "Breaking news. Mr. Dowling's lawyer, Tony Peyser, made a statement ten minutes ago—"

Sarah stared at the radio as if it were a person, listening to Lisa Kerz saying that Mr. Dowling's lawyer had gone live on KQED asking for help from the people of San Francisco. She ripped her eyes back to the road just in time to miss the guardrail.

"Okay, now here's the statement, hot off the wire," Van Buren added. "Says here, quoting Mr. Peyser, 'Mr. Dowling is offering a fifty-thousand-dollar reward for information leading to the arrest of whoever killed Casey Dowling.'"

Sarah saw her exit ramp rushing toward the car, jerked the steering wheel without signaling, and left rubber on the roadway as she made the turn. Once off the freeway, she drove without seeing, eventually finding herself in the parking lot at Booker T. Washington High.

Sarah shut off the car, grabbed her backpack, and headed through the red iron gates and into the main building, entering the teacher's lounge for her customary pick-me-up before facing the day.

The bell had rung. The lounge was nearly empty except for one person: Heidi Meyer, who was standing by the coffee machine, stirring her cup. Sarah called out, "Hey, Heidi."

"Hey, yourself. Whoa. You okay, Sarah?"

"Bah. Trevor's a bastard. Heard enough?"

Heidi put down her cup and opened her arms to give Sarah a hug. Sarah walked into the embrace and was enveloped by the scent of lilacs. She buried her face in the soft cloud of Heidi's red hair and just held on.

Could Heidi hear her blood roaring? God. The implications of what she'd just heard were inescapable. The police would be seriously focused on finding Sarah, and they'd be looking to charge her for killing Casey Dowling. That was just insane.

"We're late to class," Heidi said, rubbing Sarah's back, "and the monsters will be revolting."

"As always." Sarah laughed.

Heidi gave Sarah a peck on the lips—and Sarah kissed Heidi back, but harder and with feeling, Heidi's sweet mouth opening under hers as Sarah put her whole heart into it.

If only she could tell Heidi everything.

Chapter **18**

THE MORNING AFTER their murders, Barbara Ann and Darren Benton, along with Casey Dowling, were chilling in the morgue while Conklin and I stared at each other across our overloaded desks, not knowing whether to spit or go blind.

We were working the Dowling case because Jacobi had been absolutely clear when he said, "Dowling trumps Benton. Dowling trumps everything." Because Casey Dowling was a high-profile victim and the Bentons were not.

I told Jacobi that the lunatic killer who'd left a message in the Bentons' RAV4 made me feel like I'd put my finger in a live electric socket. That I was sure their killer was signaling a pattern in the making. That Conklin and I should be on the Benton case now, full-time.

Jacobi showed me his palms. *What do you want from me? No manpower. No budget. I want to keep my job. Do what I tell you.*

Conklin looked fresh, his brown eyes sparkling in the gloom of the bull pen, his shining brown hair falling across his forehead as we studied Stolen Property's case notes on Hello Kitty and scoured crime scene photos of the Dowlings' master bedroom.

I was uploading Clapper's footage of the scene when Cindy Thomas blew through the gates and headed toward Conklin and me.

"Look at this!" she shouted, her blond bed-spring curls bouncing, blue lightning flashing in her eyes.

She was waving the *Oakland Tribune,* the smaller, foxier tabloid that competes with the *Chronicle.* The headline read, "Hello Kitty Kills." Because Cindy had named this cat burglar and had reported on his heists, she considered him *hers*.

"Everyone's on my story now," she said, swiveling her fierce gaze from me to Conklin and back to me again. "Give me a break, please. I need something that the *Trib* doesn't have."

"We've got nothing," I said. "Wish we did."

"Rich?" she said to my partner.

Cindy is four years younger than I, more a little sister to me than my actual little sister. I love her, and even though she fights me, she also uses her keen intuition and bulldog tenacity to help me solve homicides. That's in the plus column.

Cindy pulled over a chair, triangulating me and Conklin. It was a neat visual metaphor, and I didn't like it.

"Why would Hello Kitty kill Casey Dowling?" she asked. "Kitty has never been violent. Why would he even be carrying a gun when armed robbery would get him life?"

"We're working the case, Cindy," I said. "Jeez. We haven't stopped. I got all of two hours in the rack last night—"

"Rich?" Cindy cocked her head like a little yellow bird.

"Exactly what Lindsay said. We've got nothing. No prints. No gun. No witnesses."

"Usual deal," Cindy said. She batted her eyelashes at Conklin and gave him her best come-hither stare. "Off the record."

Conklin waited a beat, then said, "What if Casey knew the intruder?"

Cindy leaped up, hugged Conklin around the neck, kissed him on the mouth, and then flew out of the squad room.

"BYE, CINDY," I called after her.

Conklin laughed.

Chapter 19

"I'M GOING TO see Claire," I told my partner.

"Stay in touch," he said.

I ran down three flights and worked my way through the Hall's crowded lobby, out the back door, and down the breezeway to the medical examiner's office.

I found Claire in the autopsy suite. She was wearing a floral shower cap and an apron over her XXL scrubs—still carrying some poundage from her pregnancy on her size-sixteen frame. I called out to her, and she looked up from the body of Barbara Ann Benton, who was lying eviscerated on the table.

"You just missed Cindy," Claire said, putting Barbara Ann's liver onto a scale.

"No, I didn't. She stormed the squad room. Got Conklin into a lip-lock. Promised him favors in exchange for a headline, and he lapped it up. What'd she get out of you?"

"Breaking news. Casey Dowling was shot to death. Cindy has the best job, doesn't she? She can focus on her one and only story and still have time to get it on with Inspector Hottie."

"Anything interesting on Barbara Ann Benton?" I asked, staring into the dead woman's abdominal cavity, hoping to head off a sore subject. To be precise, it was hard keeping Cindy out of confidential police business—and *I* wasn't sleeping with her.

"No postmortem surprises," said Claire. "Mrs. Benton took two slugs. Either one of them could have killed her, but the shot to the chest is the cause of death."

"And the baby?"

"Cause of death, a nine millimetre through the temporal lobe. Calling it a homicide. That's signed, stamped, and official. The slugs are at the lab."

Claire asked her assistant to finish with Barbara Ann, then stripped off her gloves and mask and walked me out of the autopsy suite and into her office. She took the swivel chair, and I slumped into the seat across from her desk. She pulled two bottles of water out of the fridge and handed one to me.

Claire has a picture on her desk, and I turned it around so I could scrutinize the four of us on the front steps of the Hall of Justice. There was Yuki, all suited up, her dark hair parted in the middle, falling in two glossy wings to her chin; Cindy was grinning, her slightly overlapping front teeth drawing attention to how pretty she really is; and then there was Claire, buxom and beautiful in her midforties.

And there I was, towering over them all at five ten, wearing my blond hair in a ponytail and sporting a dead-serious look on my face. The thing is, I think of myself as lighthearted. I wonder where I got that idea.

"What's wrong, Lindsay?"

"You don't always get what you want," I said, sort of smiling.

"The Benton case? Or the other thing?"

"Both. Listen, I'm supervising Chi on Benton, but he's the primary."

"I know. And you know Paul Chi will kill himself to solve the case."

I nodded. "Tell me what you've got on Casey Dowling."

"Her assailant used a forty-four."

"You're kidding."

"I know. What's a burglar doing with a cannon when a cute little nine would do? Lab didn't get a hit from the database."

"That was quick," I said.

"I leaned on Clapper to rush it, and now I have to name my next child after him."

"Clapper Washburn. Rough handle for a child."

Claire laughed, then sobered. "Maybe I've got something."

"Don't make me beg."

"When I did the rape kit on Casey Dowling, I found evidence of sexual intercourse. The little fishes were still swimming."

Chapter 20

WHEN I GOT back to my desk, Conklin said, "While you were out, seventy-two people called with tips about Casey Dowling's murder. Look." Brenda came over and dropped several pink message squares on his desk. "Ten more."

"What did I miss?"

"Dowling's lawyer went on the air, said he's putting up fifty grand for info leading to the arrest of Casey Dowling's killer."

"So here's the question, Rich. Is Dowling completely right to offer a reward? Or is he jamming us up with wacko tipsters so we can't work the case?"

I called Yuki to discuss the possibility of getting a warrant for Dowling's phone and computer records when Jacobi pulled a chair into the center of the bull pen, straddled it, and called the squad to attention.

I was struck again by how crappy he looked. Jacobi is a veteran of the force: he's served roughly twenty years in Homicide, a survivor of both physical attacks and life's vicissitudes. So what was so special that it was bothering the hell out of him?

Jacobi nodded at me, then swung his head and took in the rest of the day shift: Inspectors Chi, McNeil, Lemke, Samuels, and Conklin, and a couple of guys from the swing shift who'd been drafted to help us out. I guessed Jacobi was thinking about how few of us there were, how many cases we were working, and how small a number of those cases we would ever solve.

Jacobi asked Chi to make his report on Benton.

Chi stood, five feet eleven inches of canny brainiac. He reported that he and his partner had done a follow-up with Richard Benton, that Benton's alibi checked out, and that Barbara Ann Benton's life insurance wouldn't pay out enough to bury her.

Said Chi, "The surveillance tape from the

garage is grainy. The shooter was wearing a cap. He kept his head down, but from what we can see of his neck, we think he's white. Seems like he said something to the victim before he shot her and the baby. He took nothing, but maybe he panicked. It still looks like a holdup that went wrong."

Jacobi asked him the questions that were on all our minds: "Why did the shooter kill the kid? And, Jesus, Paul, what's WCF?"

"There's no WCF in the database, Lieutenant. It's not a gang or a known terrorist organization. Found about thirty phone listings for first names starting with 'W,' last names starting with 'F,' and six with the middle initial 'C.' We're running them down."

Next into the buzz saw was me.

I briefed the squad on the whole nine yards of the nothing we had on the death of Casey Dowling, saying that we were looking at five recent burglaries with the same MO.

"In all six incidents, the homeowners were home, and no one ever saw the burglar. This time there's a fatality," I said, "and maybe a witness. A ten-year-old neighbor saw someone in black running from the scene. Right now, it looks like the victim surprised the burglar, and he shot her."

Jacobi nodded, and then he dropped the bomb.

"The chief called me in this morning and said it would be more efficient to combine our unit with the Northern Division Homicide Section."

"What does that mean, 'combine'?" I asked, dumbfounded at the idea of doubling up in our twenty-by-thirty-foot work space.

"The thinking upstairs is to have more bodies working the cases, more collaborative problem solving, and, hell, probably a new chain of command."

So that's why Jacobi looked like he'd been dragged behind a truck. His job was in danger, and that would affect us all.

"It's not a done deal," Jacobi said. "Let's close these cases. I can't fight if we're losing."

The meeting ended with a collective sigh, after which Jacobi invited me and Conklin to join him in what we jokingly call his corner office: a small, glass-walled cell with a window overlooking the freeway.

Conklin took the side chair and I leaned

against the door frame, assessing the horizontal grooves that had appeared overnight on Jacobi's forehead.

"Dowling didn't have a heart attack," Jacobi told us. "Chest pains. Rapid breathing. It's being called a stress attack. Could be. It fits. Or maybe he was acting. Maybe this time he'll get that Oscar. Meanwhile, he's just been released from the hospital."

I told Jacobi that the ME's report said Casey Dowling had had sex before she died. "We're on our way to see Dowling."

"I'll be waiting by the phone," Jacobi said.

Chapter 21

MARCUS DOWLING OPENED his door and showed us to a sitting room decorated to the hilt with English-style roll-arm sofas, Flow Blue platters on the walls, and Foo dogs on the mantel. Mayfair meets the City on the Bay.

A woman in a black dress, not introduced, offered beverages and quietly left the room, returning with bottled water for Conklin and me, Chivas for our host.

I said, "Mr. Dowling, tell us again what happened last night."

He said, "Jesus Christ, I told you everything, didn't I? I thought you were coming here to tell *me* something."

Conklin, who is a sensational good cop to my

badass bitch, said, "We apologize, sir. The thing is, your telling us what happened again might trigger a memory or a new thought about who did this."

Dowling nodded, leaned back in his leather chair, and put down a healthy swig of scotch. "The Devereaus had gone," he said. "As I told the other officer, I was putting things into the sink—"

"The lady who brought the beverages," I interrupted. "She wasn't here to help?"

"Vangy only works days. She has a child."

Dowling repeated how his wife had gone upstairs before him, how he heard shots, how he found his wife on the floor, not breathing, and how he'd called the police.

I said, "Mr. Dowling, I noticed last night that your hair was wet. You took a shower before the police came?"

He grunted and gripped his glass. I was watching for a tell—a guilty look—and I thought I saw it. "I was devastated. I stood weeping in the shower because I didn't know what else to do."

"And your clothes, sir?" Conklin asked.

"My clothes?"

"Mr. Dowling, let me be honest with you," Conklin said. "We know you're a victim here, but there are certain protocols. We take your clothes to the lab, and it puts down any questions that might come up later."

Dowling gave Conklin a furious look and called out, "Van-gy! Take Inspector Conklin upstairs and give him whatever he wants."

When Conklin and the housekeeper left the room, I asked, "Mr. Dowling, when was the last time you had intimate relations with your wife?"

"My God. What are you getting at?"

"Someone had sex with your wife," I said, pressing on. "If it was her killer, he left evidence that could help us—"

"Casey had sex with *me!*" Dowling shouted. "We made love before dinner. Now what exactly does that tell you?"

Fifteen minutes later, Conklin and I left Dowling's house with a printout of his phone contact list, a cheek swab, and all the unlaundered clothing he owned. Presumably that included what he was wearing when his wife was shot.

"I took everything in the clothes hamper and whatever was on the hook behind the bathroom door," Conklin said as we walked out to the car. "If he shot her, we'll have gunpowder. We'll have blood spatter. We'll have *him*."

Chapter 22

IT WAS THE end of a very long day when Claire and I came in from the dark street into Susie's, with its splashy sponge-painted walls, spicy aromas, and the plinking drumbeat of the steel band.

Cindy and Yuki were holding down our favorite table in the back room, Yuki in her best go-to-court suit while Cindy had swapped out her denims for something flirty in baby-blue chiffon under a short, cream-colored jacket. They were putting away plantain chips and beer and were in deep conversation about the Dowling case.

Claire and I slid into the booth as Cindy said, "Casey Dowling owned a twenty-karat canary diamond ring worth a million bucks. Known as the Sun of Ceylon. Maybe she fought to keep it. What do you think, Linds? Possible motive for Hello Kitty to go ballistic?"

"Casey didn't have any defensive wounds," said Claire.

"And she didn't scream for her husband," I added.

I poured beer from the pitcher for Claire and myself, then asked Cindy, "Where'd you get that info about the diamond?"

"I've got my sources. But I wouldn't get too excited, Linds. That rock will have been chopped into pebbles by now."

"Maybe," I said to Cindy. "Listen, I have a thought. Since you know who's who, maybe you could run your fingers through the social register, flag anyone young and athletic enough to do second-story jobs."

Yuki asked, "You're thinking Hello Kitty is high-society?"

"Rich does," Cindy and I said in unison.

Yuki tucked her hair behind her ears. "If Kitty travels with that crowd, he'd know Casey had this huge yellow diamond, and if she recognized him—"

"Yeah, I admit, it makes sense," I said. "There was a forced-window entry into the Dowling bedroom, identical to the other five break-ins. There's a witness who saw someone making a getaway on foot. Clapper says there's no gunpowder or blood spatter on Dowling's clothing. So if Casey knew Kitty—"

And then Claire thumped the table with her fist. Chips jumped. Beer sloshed. She got everyone's complete attention.

"I'm sorry, but the Benton killings give me the creeps. WCF. What's that? It's crazy. Sinister crazy. Mystery gunpowder stippling. Mystery motive. Dead baby, shot execution-style.

"So let me be clear: I don't care whose case it is, and I know it's not right to care more about one murder victim over another. I said I'm sorry, and I am, but this dead baby hurts me. Deeply. And now I'm going home to my man and my little girl."

Chapter 23

YUKI PAID THE tab and told Lorraine to keep the change. She realized suddenly that she'd never given the others her news. Usually girls' night out at Susie's was laughing and venting and dinner. But tonight everyone got intense and then —they were gone.

Yuki stood up, buttoned her jacket, and walked past the kitchen and into the main room. Her hand was on the front door handle when, on impulse, she turned and walked back to the bar.

The bartender had dark curly hair, an easy smile, and a name tag stitched onto the fabric of his wild-printed shirt.

"Miles?"

"That's my name," he told her. "Wait. I've seen

you before. You and your friends — beer and margaritas, right?"

"I'm Yuki Castellano," she said, shaking his hand. "What do you drink to celebrate a good day in court?"

"You beat a traffic ticket?"

Yuki laughed.

"Do that again," Miles said. "I think the sun just came out."

"I'm a prosecutor," she said. "Things turned out fine for the good guys today. So what do you think? What am I drinking?"

"Classic. Traditional. Always in style."

"Perfect," Yuki said as Miles poured champagne. "You know, today was stupendous, except for the one stone in my shoe."

"Tell me about it."

Yuki ordered a spicy crab salad, then told Miles about the case against Jo-Jo Johnson and how the victim, the dead Dr. Harris, was a very bad dude but that Jo-Jo was worse. He'd let the man die in his own vomit over the course of fifteen hours.

"Should have taken the jury about five minutes to find Jo-Jo guilty," Miles said.

"Shoulda, but it took a day and a half. Jo-Jo's

lawyer is very smooth, and Jo-Jo is disarmingly simple. Like, you could believe that he really didn't know that Harris was dying if you totally squinted your eyes and put your common sense in the deep freeze."

"So it's terrific that you won."

"Yeah. I've been at this a couple of years. I've had a lot of losses."

"So you didn't say. What's the stone in your shoe?"

"His name's Jeff Asher. Opposing counsel. He came up to me after his client was taken out in handcuffs and said, 'Congratulations on your win, Yuki. What is that? One in a row?'"

"He's a sore loser," the bartender said. "You hurt him, Yuki. Definitely. Guess what? Your champagne's on the house."

"Thanks, Miles. Yeah. You're right. He's a sore loser."

"Bartenders never lie," Miles said.

Yuki laughed.

"Here comes the sun," he said.

Chapter 24

CINDY'S BLOUSE WAS a cloud of silk chiffon in the rear foot well of Rich Conklin's car. Her skirt was rolled up to her waist, and her panty hose dangled from one foot. She was damned uncomfortable, but she wouldn't change a thing.

She rested her hand on Rich's chest, damp from the romp, and felt his heart thudding. He pulled her in tight and kissed her.

"What a concert," he said.

"Tremendous rhythm section," she said, both of them cracking up.

They were parked in an alley near the Embarcadero, where Rich had pulled the car into the shadows because Cindy's hand on his leg had made it impossible to wait.

He said now, "I can almost hear the cop knocking on the window with his flashlight, saying, 'Hey, what's going on in there?'"

"And you putting your shield to the glass, saying, 'Officer down.'"

Conklin started laughing. "I don't have any idea where my shield is. You are so witchy, Cin, and I mean that in the nicest possible way."

She gave him a sly smile and ran her hand over his naked chest and slid it down, then kissed him, starting up his breathing, and there he was, hard again, kissing her, pulling her on top of him.

"Keep your head down," he panted. "Headlights."

Cindy leaned over and fastened her mouth to his, broke away, raised and lowered her hips, and worked him with her eyes open, watching his face change, letting him see her, really see her. She slid up and away from him, and he put his hands around her waist and pulled her down on him, hard.

"You drive me crazy, Cin."

She put her cheek down on his collarbone, letting him drive the action, feeling secure and at risk the whole time, a powerfully explosive combination. And then she was calling his name, and he released himself into her.

"Oh my God," she said, panting, then fading, wanting to fall asleep in Rich's arms. But there was something bothering her, something she'd never felt it was okay to ask him until now.

"Rich?"

"Want to go for three?" he asked her.

"Dare you," she said, and they both laughed, and then she just blurted it out. "Rich, have you ever—"

"Maybe, once or twice before."

"No, listen. Did you ever do it with Lindsay?"

"No. No. C'mon, Cindy. She's my *partner*."

"So that's what—illegal?"

"I think my arm's dead," he said to her.

Cindy shifted her weight, and then there was a whole lot of looking for articles of clothing and deciding where to spend the night.

She'd spoiled the mood, Cindy thought, buttoning her blouse. And she wasn't even sure he'd told her the truth.

Chapter 25

PETE GORDON WAS standing in the kitchen, whipping up some instant mashed potatoes on the stove while watching the baseball game on the undercabinet TV, when his wife came through the door.

"Whatcha burning?" she asked.

"Listen, princess, I don't need your frickin' cooking tips, and now you made me miss that pitch."

"So why don't you rewind it, sweetie?"

"Do you see a DVR in here? Do you?"

"Sorry, Mr. Cranky. I'm just saying you could save that if you put a little milk in it and turned down the flame."

"For Christ's sake," Pete said, switching off the

gas, scraping the potatoes into a bowl. "You just can't let me have a single simple pleasure, can you?"

"Well, I have a surprise."

"Let's hear it." He dialed up the volume and ate the potatoes standing in front of the set. He spit into the sink as the food burned his mouth, glancing up in time to see the opposing team crossing the plate. "NO!" he screamed. "Goddamn Giants. How could they lose this game?"

"My aunt said she'd like to take all of us out to dinner tomorrow. Special treat — on her."

"Yippee. Sounds like fun. Your fat-assed aunt and all of us around a table at the Olive Garden."

"Pete."

No answer.

"Pete," she said, reaching up and turning off the television. He swung his head around and glared at her.

"It's not about you, handsome. It's about the kids having dinner with their family."

"You guys can get along without me. Just wing it, princess," Petey said, not quite believing it when she took the remote off the counter, jammed it down the disposal, and hit the switch.

"Go to hell, Petey," she said as the machine gnawed on the plastic. "No, I really mean it."

Pete shut off the grinder and watched his fucking wife flounce out of the room. He reran the last scene in his mind, only this time he put wifey's hand into the grinder. Yeah. The metal teeth chomping through muscle and bone as she screamed her head off.

He was going to get her.

He was going to get her and Sherry and the stink bomb one day really soon.

WCF, people. Wait for it.

Chapter 26

MY EYELIDS FLEW open at 5:52 a.m. exactly. I know because Joe has a projection clock, a high-tech gadget that shows the time and temperature in red digits on the ceiling.

I like knowing this information by simply opening my eyes. But this morning, I saw the red numerals and thought, *WCF*.

That goddamned baby-killing psycho had infiltrated my mind, and I didn't hold it against Claire one bit that she was so incensed and freaked and practically murderous herself. The insidious lipstick letters—the clue that led to nothing—were like the freight train heading toward the house when there was no place to run.

I wondered how Chi and McNeil were doing

with the phone list that matched those initials. Man, it would be great if it led to the shooter, but a killer signing his work with his actual *initials?* Forget it.

I closed my eyes, but Martha was on to me. She put her snoot on the mattress, pinned me with her gorgeous brown eyes, and started thumping her tail. Then Joe turned over. He wrapped his arms around me, brought me into a bear hug, and said, "Linds. Try to sleep." It was now 6:14.

"Okay," I said, turning away from him so that he could hold me in the hollow of his body. He was breathing softly over my shoulder, so I sent my mind back to the days when I lived in my own place on Potrero Hill. My life had been very different then, jogging with Martha most mornings, running the squad, coming home to Martha at night. I remembered the microwaved, one-dish cooking, a little too much vino, wondering when I'd hear from Joe. Wondering when I'd see him.

And then my apartment burned down.

And now Joe was living here, and I was wearing his ring. At this moment it felt almost as though he were riding along with my thoughts.

He held me closer and cupped my breasts. He got hard against me, and then he ran his hand down to my belly and pressed me to him.

As his breathing sped up, so did mine, and then he was turning me as though I were a tiny thing —a feeling that I just love. I squirmed from his touch, heating up under this new kind of loving that felt so different from the roller-coaster craziness of the time before Joe and I finally committed to a shared life.

I faced him and wrapped my arms around his neck, and he pulled my legs up to his waist, and this incredible, breathtaking moment bloomed. I waited through the tension of those long seconds before he entered me. I looked into his deep-blue eyes—and gave myself over to him.

"I love you, Blondie," he said.

I nodded because I couldn't speak. Tears were in my eyes and my throat ached as we joined together. He held me and rocked me, and I was happy. I loved this man. Our lives were finally blending in a delicious and balanced way.

So what was nagging me from a cul-de-sac in my mind? Why did I feel that I was letting myself down?

WOMEN'S MURDER CLUB

Part Two

SHOWTIME

Chapter 27

SARAH WELLS FLIPPED the chicken-fried steak in the pan and removed the garlic bread from the oven, thinking that it was all heart-attack food—or was that just wishful thinking?

The TV was on in the next room. Sarah could see it through the wall opening and could hear Helen Ross, the pretty, blond talk-show host, over the crackling of grease in the pan. Ross was sympathizing with Marcus Dowling about the pain of losing his wife.

"Come on, Helen," Sarah muttered. "Put him on the grill. Don't be a jerk."

"She was so happy," Dowling was saying. "We'd had this lovely dinner with friends. We were going on holiday, and then—this. The unimaginable."

"It *is* unimaginable," Ross said. She reached out to touch Dowling's hand. "Casey had such spirit, such charisma. We did a Red Cross fund-raiser together last year."

"There is no way to describe the agony," Dowling said. "I keep thinking, *If only I hadn't done the washing up*—"

Trevor came into the kitchen, opened the fridge, and bent to take out a beer, his girth falling over the waistband of his underwear. He popped the top, took a swig of Bud, then walked behind his wife and grabbed her ass.

"Hey," she said, moving out of his reach.

"What's with you?"

"Here," she said, handing him the tongs. "Take over, okay?"

"Where're you going?"

"I've had a tough day, Trev."

"You ought to see a doctor, you know."

"Shut up."

"Because you're on the rag all the time."

Sarah sank into the couch and turned up the volume. All she'd thought about since she stole the jewelry was Marcus Dowling, trying to understand what the hell had happened once she'd bailed out the window.

"You couldn't have known," Helen Ross was saying.

The pan slammed on the stove behind her, Trevor trying to get her attention. On the TV, Dowling was saying, "The police haven't turned up anything, and meanwhile this killer is *free*."

Sarah finally got it. She didn't know *why* he did it, but it was *he*. Dowling had killed his wife! There was no one else it could be. How convenient that Sarah had broken into his house so that he could set her up to take the fall.

Trevor said, "Chow's on, darlin'. Your Cheerios are just the way you like 'em."

Sarah turned off the TV and went to the dinette. "I'm sorry I snapped at you," she said, thinking it was better to apologize than to get him more wound up. Sometimes he could get physical. When she talked to Heidi about Trevor, they called him "Terror." It was an apt nickname.

Trevor grunted, sawed on his steak, and said, "Don't worry about it. I just wonder sometimes what you did to the sweet little girl I married."

"One of life's mysteries," she said.

"What you meant to say was, 'I'll make it up to you tonight, sweetie.' Isn't that right?"

Sarah ducked Trevor's glare and dipped her spoon into the bowl of cereal. She was going to have to step up the schedule. Maybe it wasn't right, but she was going to get rich or go to jail.

There really wasn't any other choice.

Chapter 28

SARAH WENT THROUGH the yard. Everything was dark except for the twinkle of the small light on the back porch, and where moonlight filtered through the tree limbs. The light was a signal that the back door was unlocked behind the screen.

The door swung open under Sarah's hand, and she walked quietly up to the woman who was washing some dishes in the sink. Sarah put her arms around the woman's waist and said, "Don't scream."

"Wow. You got here fast," Heidi said, spinning around.

"Terror was passed out, as usual," Sarah said, kissing Heidi, swaying with her in the dim light of the kitchen. "Where's Beastly?" she asked, referring to Heidi's husband.

Heidi reached up to a cabinet, took out two glasses, and said to Sarah, "You know what he always says. 'Anywhere but here.' Want to get the bottle out of the fridge?"

The staircase creaked under their feet, and so did the floorboards in the hallway that led past the kids' room to a dormered bedroom at the back of the second floor.

"How long can you stay?" Heidi asked. She turned up the baby monitor, then unbuttoned her pale-yellow sweater and stepped out of her jeans.

Sarah shrugged. "If he wakes up and finds me gone, what's he going to do? Call the police?"

Heidi undressed Sarah, carefully undid the oversize shirt one slow button at a time, unzipped the low-riding jeans, marveled as she ran her hands over Sarah's lean runner's body. Sarah was so strong.

"Your body is the next best thing to having a body like this myself," Heidi said.

"You're perfect. I love everything about you."

"That was my line. Get into the bed, now. Go on."

Heidi handed Sarah a glass and eased in next to her love, her sweetheart. The two women got comfortable in the iron bedstead under the eaves, Heidi putting a hand on Sarah's thigh, Sarah drawing Heidi closer under her protective arm.

"So what's on our travelogue tonight?" Heidi asked.

Sarah had a list of three places, but she had a special feeling about Palau. She told Heidi, "It's so far from anywhere. You can swim naked in these amazing grottoes. Nobody cares about who you are," she said.

"No problems with a quartet of two women, two kids?"

"We'll say we're sisters. You're widowed."

"Oh, because the family resemblance is so strong?"

"Sisters-in-law, then."

"Okay. And about the language? What is it?"

"Palauan, of course. But they speak English, too."

"All right, then. To life in Palau," Heidi said, touching Sarah's glass with hers. They sipped and kissed with their eyes open, then the glasses were put aside and they reached for each other, Heidi listening to the baby monitor, Sarah with an eye to the window, fear driving their passion into high gear.

As Heidi stripped off Sarah's panties, Sarah was thinking, *We can escape as soon as the last jobs are done. As soon as the jewels are sold.*

"Sarah?"

"I'm here, Heidi. Thinking of the future."

"Come to me now."

Sarah had a sudden thought. She should tell Heidi about that woman and child she'd heard about who were killed in a parking garage, warn her to be very careful—but a second later, the thought faded and another came into focus.

She would sell everything but that yellow stone. One day soon, she'd give it to Heidi.

Chapter 29

IT WAS EIGHT in the morning when Jacobi dragged his chair into the center of the room and called us together. Yuki sat beside me. Claire stood behind Jacobi, arms crossed over her chest, just as emotionally invested in the young, deceased Darren Benton as Yuki was in Casey Dowling.

I noticed the stranger sitting in a metal chair in the corner: suntanned white male, midthirties, narrow blue eyes, sun-bleached blond hair pulled back and knotted with a rubber band. He was maybe five ten, 160 pounds, and he looked buff from the way his blazer stretched across his biceps.

This guy was a cop. A cop I didn't know.

Jacobi picked up where we'd left off the day before. Chi reported on the Benton case, saying that there was no match to the slugs found in the Bentons' bodies. He noted that the stippling pattern was still unidentified but that Dr. Washburn had sent photos out to the FBI.

Chi jiggled the coins in his pocket and looked uncomfortable when he said that the lipstick used to write the letters "WCF" was a common, inexpensive drugstore brand.

Bottom line: they had nothing.

I stood and briefed the squad, saying that we were going over the Dowlings' phone records and that there were many dozens of numbers that came up repeatedly on both lists. I said that we had found nothing unusual in either of the Dowlings' bank-account records.

"Casey Dowling owned a very distinctive piece of jewelry," I continued. "We're working on that, and we haven't turned up anything at all on Hello Kitty. All bright ideas are welcome. Anyone wants to work the psycho tip line, raise your hand."

Of course, no one did.

The meeting was wrapping up when Jacobi

said, "Everyone say hello to Sergeant Jackson Brady."

The cop sitting in the back lifted his hand in a wave and looked around as he was introduced.

"Jack Brady is a new transfer," Jacobi said. "He's put in a dozen years with Miami PD, most of those in Homicide. Chief Tracchio has attached him to our unit as a pinch hitter in the short-term, pending his permanent assignment. God knows we need the help. Please make him feel welcome."

Jacobi dismissed us, and Jackson Brady came over to my desk and put out his hand. I shook it, told him my name, and introduced him to Conklin.

Brady nodded and said he'd heard about the firebugs, a case involving two boys who set fire to houses, killing the residents—a case Conklin and I had closed.

I saw Brady's sharp blue eyes raking the small squad room as I talked. I turned to see Claire speaking with Jacobi, Cindy huddling with Yuki, the TV in the corner of the room showing Marcus Dowling still chatting up the press.

"The more they talk, the less I believe them,"

Brady said, jutting his chin toward the images of Dowling.

"We've been working the case for a few days," I said. "We're just getting our teeth into it."

"I heard your report, Sergeant," Brady said. "You don't have a clue."

Chapter 30

ERNIE COOPER'S PAWNSHOP is wedged between a Chinese fast-food restaurant and a smoke shop on Valencia, at the heart of the Mission. Casey Dowling's high-ticket jewelry was out of Ernie Cooper's league, but Cooper was retired from the SFPD and had offered help anytime we needed him.

Today, the hulking ex-cop's frame was filling up a faded art deco fan chair on the sidewalk outside his shop. His gray hair was braided down his back, iPod cords dangled from his ears, an open racing form was on his lap, and there was the bulge of a handgun under his aloha shirt.

Cooper grinned when he saw us and stood up to shake Conklin's hand and mine.

"We're working a burglary that turned into a murder," I told him.

"Movie star's wife? I read about that," he said. "Have a seat."

I pulled up a toy trunk, and Conklin balanced his rump on a bamboo bar stool. Cooper said, "Fill me in."

I handed him the folder of insurance photos, and he flipped through them, stopping often to take in the sapphires in platinum settings, the chains of diamonds, and then the real show-stopper — the yellow diamond ring looking like a pasha's cushion set in a throne of pavé diamonds.

"Man alive," Cooper said. He flipped the photo over and read the specs of the piece. "Appraised at a million. And I'm betting it's worth every penny."

"It's one of a kind, right?" Conklin asked him.

"Oh, sure," Cooper said. "A twenty-karat diamond of any kind is rare. But a canary diamond? The setting alone says it's an original. I wonder why it's not signed."

"So what would you do if you stole this?" I asked.

"Well, I wouldn't shop it here, that's for sure.

I'd hand it off to a flying fence, take my ten percent, and be done."

"Flying fence" was a new term for me. I asked Ernie to explain.

"A flying fence is like the regular kind, except he takes possession of the goods immediately, catches a flight to LA or New York or another jewelry-laundering hub, and is in the air within an hour or so of the robbery."

"And then what?"

"The route fans out to anywhere. In the case of this ring, maybe it's been sold as is, but not in this country. Probably on the finger of a young lady in Dubai as we speak."

Cooper drummed his fingers on the folder. I thought I could see a lightbulb going on over his head.

"You know, there was a flying fence who took a bullet in New York a couple of months ago. Yeah, Maury Green. He specialized in high-priced gems. Normally he'd be the guy you'd go to with a hot rock like this."

"He was killed?"

"Yep, on the spot. Green was taking possession of a haul, and the cops tagged the guy who was making the drop. Can't remember his name, but he was wanted for armed robbery. So anyway, the mope pulled a gun, and Maury Green got caught in the cross fire. That put a break in the supply chain.

"You know," Cooper said, "if your Hello Kitty was using Green to fence his goods, he may be stuck with this million-dollar chunk of yellow ice for a while. Could be your cat's up a tree, doesn't know how to get down."

Chapter 31

YUKI HUGGED THE tanned, graceful woman who opened the door.

"God, it's been what, six years? You look the same!" Sue Emdin said to Yuki, the whole time looking at her like *Gee, I haven't heard from you since graduation, so what's this about?*

As they walked through the house, Yuki and Sue chatted about their days at Boalt Law, and once they were comfortably seated outside on the wraparound porch with iced tea and cookies, Yuki brought up Casey Dowling and how she'd died.

"You want to talk about Casey *officially?*" Sue asked.

"Uh-huh. But what's the difference, Sue? Casey

is dead, and we owe it to her to help catch her killer."

"Understand, both Marc and Casey are my friends," Sue said. "I don't want to say anything behind Marc's back."

"I do understand, and right now, this is between us," Yuki said. "If you know something, you have to tell me, and you have to let me use my judgment. You'd expect the same from me."

"All right, all right. But try to keep me out of it, okay? When was the last time I asked you for a favor?"

Yuki laughed, and Sue joined her, saying, "Never, right?"

"This is the first time."

"Between you and me, Casey told me she thought Marcus was having an affair. There. I said it."

"Did she have any proof? Did she suspect someone in particular? Did she confront Marcus?"

"Slow down. One question at a time," Sue said.

"Sorry. Backing up, now. Did Casey have any proof that Marcus was screwing around?"

"No, but she was suspicious. Marc's always

been a letch. He put his hand on my butt once or twice. Hell, he's a movie star. But Casey said, and I quote, 'He's gone off me.' Meaning he didn't have the hots for her anymore. That's all the proof she had — none — and at the same time, she was alarmed."

"Did she confront him?"

"Yuki, you're not thinking Marc shot Casey?"

"Not at all. He's clean. But it helps to know if there was trouble in the marriage."

"I'm a lawyer, too, remember, and I'm telling you Marcus didn't do it. Marc totally loved Casey. He thought she was a riot. He said he'd never had a boring moment in the four years he was married to her. Ben and I went over to Marc's house last night, and he was devastated. He said he was dying from grief. And even if he was fooling around, he wouldn't have left Casey. He certainly wouldn't have — I can't even say it."

"Would Casey have divorced him?"

Sue Emdin sighed. "I don't know. Maybe. She told me that if she found out he was cheating, she'd leave him."

"When did she say that?"

"Tuesday night."

"Sue, Casey was killed on *Wednesday*."

"Look somewhere else, Yuki. Trust me on this. It was that cat burglar. Marcus didn't do it."

Chapter 32

PETE GORDON WAS hunting along the Embarcadero, the eastern roadway that fronts the bay, running from 2nd and King, past the Ferry Building, and north under the San Francisco–Oakland Bay Bridge, an artery traveled by locals and tourists alike. People flowed around him on foot, on bike, on skateboard, as the setting sun licked at the indigo sky.

Pete had picked his target outside the Ferry Building, a reed-thin blonde wearing a hooded black Windbreaker over her long black skirt, her clothes billowing and snapping in the breeze. Made him think of a woman in a burka.

The thin blonde was pushing a kiddo in a stroller, a calm child in pink who seemed to be

135

taking in the travelers getting off the ferry and fanning out through the marketplace.

Pete followed the black-cloaked blonde through the farmer's market, watching her pick out one loaf of bread, one head of lettuce, and one fish fillet. He stayed on her tail as she left the market, plastic bags looped over her wrists, not talking to her daughter, who in some way seemed to be in charge.

When his target got to the intersection of Market and Spear, she headed toward the BART entrance. She tilted the stroller up and stepped onto the down escalator, and Pete knew it was time. He gripped his gun in his right hand, the whole of it buried in his pocket, and followed her off the moving stairway.

"Miss? Ma'am?" he shouted. The third time he called her, she whipped her head around and shot him a look: *What is it?*

He ducked his head and gave her a shy smile. "I'm supposed to meet a friend at the corner of California. I've, uh, gotten lost."

The woman stared at him and said, "I can't help you," and pushed the stroller out from the arch toward the entrance to the underground.

"Hey, thanks, lady!" Pete yelled out. "I appreciate the fucking time of day."

Hands jammed in his pockets, Pete continued north. It wasn't over yet. He wondered if his expression had given him away. Had he looked too eager? Too raw?

It hadn't been this way in Iraq. And he wouldn't mess up here.

He was steady. He was focused. He had a mission.

And he *would* accomplish it.

Chapter 33

AS PETE WALKED into the crosswind, he was remembering PFC Kenneth Marshall's last day.

Pete had been in the lead vehicle on the dusty road just outside Haditha, his men in a caravan behind him. They were within forty meters of a cluster of houses when the car bomb exploded, blowing Corporal Lennar out of the last vehicle in the line, separating Kenny Marshall from his legs.

Pete loved Kenny like a brother. He was a smart kid with dimples and a picture of Jesus inside his helmet. He played kick-the-can with the enemy kiddos, gave them rations, believed in the mission — to bring freedom to Iraq. Kenny liked to say that when it was his time, God would find him wherever he was.

After God called Kenny, after the IED killed this good American son and soldier, after the troops in Captain Peter Gordon's command came out of their crouches, they looked to Pete for orders. It was easy. He did it by the book. His book.

Pete was sure he knew who had remotely triggered the IED. They were in the car behind the Humvee that Kenny had been driving. The next minutes were so vivid, he could smell the cordite and the dust and the fear even now. He could still hear his enemies scream as he shot them.

Now, on this cool evening in San Francisco, Pete Gordon gripped the gun inside his jacket pocket as he stalked the Embarcadero. He came to an alley between Sansome and Battery that was set up with plastic tables and chairs. A young mother was cleaning up after eating there with her bawler.

Petey followed Young Mom and her kiddo into the mall at the ground level of 1 EC, past the pastry shop and the Italian restaurant, up the escalator to the movie theater that stood apart and alone, anchoring the dead end at the western part of the second floor.

Mom was sitting on a bench, gazing at the movie posters, combing her baby's hair with her fingers. It was between shows, and they had the place to themselves.

Young Mom turned to Petey when he called out, "Ma'am, I'm sorry, could you help me, please? I'm totally lost."

Chapter 34

BY THE TIME I was called to the scene, the cruisers and the ambulances were parked all along Battery and Clay. I ran my Explorer onto the sidewalk and braked next to Jacobi's Hyundai, then grabbed one of the uniforms who was doing crowd control at the western entrance to the mall.

"Second floor, Sergeant," the uni told me. "Outside the movie theater."

I called Jacobi and he answered his phone, saying, "Come up, Boxer. And hold on to your dinner."

Moviegoers who'd been sent out through a back exit had returned to the front entrance, joining commuters and office workers and tourists who had gathered ten deep outside the entrance to 1 EC.

I held up my badge and edged through the crowd, fending off questions that I wouldn't answer if I could. A uniform opened the glass doors for me, and I entered the mall, a stretch of shops bearing famous logos, now unnaturally empty of shoppers.

The escalators had been turned off and crime scene tape stretched across the whole western wing of the mall, so I stooped under the tape and loped up the stilled mechanical stairs. Jacobi was waiting for me at the top of the escalator, and I could see from his face how bad it was going to be before I even got near the bodies on the red carpet.

I saw the mother first. She'd fallen onto her back. Her pale-blue cardigan was black over her heart from the two shots to the center mass, and she'd taken another gunshot wound to the head. I reached over and closed her sightless eyes.

Only then could I bear to look at the small, still figure lying near her.

Damn it, he'd killed the child.

This scene was a horror, and even as I recoiled

from the brutality, I was struck by how methodical these shootings had been. They had been impersonal, dead-on shots fired at close range.

Jacobi stepped aside and I circled the body of the child in the capsized stroller, a boy under the age of one. I didn't need to say to Jacobi that it was obvious these killings and the ones in the Stonestown garage were the work of the same killer.

But where was his signature? Where were the letters "WCF"?

Jacobi dropped the young mother's wallet into an evidence bag. "This is Judy Kinski. She had forty dollars in small bills. Two charge cards. Library card. She would have been twenty-six years old next week. McNeil is contacting her next of kin."

"Witnesses?" I asked. "Someone had to see this go down."

"Chi is talking to the ticket seller. Come with me."

Chapter 35

THE GIRL IN the movie-theater manager's office was crying into her hands. She looked up when I entered the tiny space. Paul Chi introduced me to the pale young woman and said, "This is Robin Rose. She may have seen the shooter."

"Is my mother here?" Robin asked.

Jacobi said, "She's on her way. As soon as she arrives, we'll escort you down."

"I didn't see the shootings," the girl said between sobs. "I was opening the booth for the seven o'clock show."

Chi handed her a wad of tissues and told her it was all right, to take her time.

"I didn't hear anything," she said, blowing her nose. "But when I rolled up the window..."

I could see it through her eyes. The last moments of her innocence, opening the cash drawer, checking the ticket feed, rolling up the metal security window, expecting—what? A couple of people wanting to buy their tickets early?

"I didn't believe it at first," Robin told us. "I thought it was some kind of alternative advertising for an upcoming show. Then I realized that those people were *real*. That they were *dead*."

"Did you see anyone near the bodies?" I asked.

She nodded and said, "He must've heard the window go up. He met my eyes for a fraction of a second. I saw the gun, so I ducked down."

The man Robin Rose saw was a white male, wearing a blue-and-white baseball jacket and a cap pulled down over his eyes. She didn't think she could describe him, but she would try. Same with his gun. And she didn't see which exit he took out of the mall.

Maybe he'd taken the skywalk over to another of the malls in the Embarcadero Center, or he could just as easily have gone down the escalator and out onto the street.

I asked Robin if she'd come in to the station to

look at surveillance tape, and then I left the manager's office with Jacobi. He was putting out an APB on a white male in a blue-and-white baseball jacket when Claire stomped up the escalator with her chief assistant, Bunny Ellis, behind her.

Claire wore a furious look as she moved in on the victims' bodies with her Minolta. I stood next to her as she said to me, "Lookit. Same weird stippling, Lindsay. Same point-blank shooting. Same bastard kid killer. Was anything stolen?"

"Mom's wallet was full."

It was Claire who saw the writing on the underside of the stroller.

I stared at the letters as cameras flashed in a stroboscopic frenzy. The message was written in lipstick. The signature was the same — but different.

FWC

"What the hell?" I said to Claire. "Not WCF? Now it's FWC?"

"You ask me, Lindsay? This guy isn't leaving clues. He's purely fucking with us."

Chapter 36

OUR PINCH HITTER, Jackson Brady, said he'd taken workshops at the FBI headquarters in Quantico.

"I spent two full summers learning to profile serial killers. That doesn't make me a pro, but I have educated opinions."

Jacobi commandeered a conference room in the Crimes Against Persons Division, and we all sat around the chipped fake-wood table, looking at Brady. Paul Chi told Brady what we'd gathered from the first scene and the latest, and Brady took notes.

All eyes were on him when he told us, "Killing children is reactive, maybe to a bad childhood, or it's possible this killer is so dead inside, he just wastes the kids because they're witnesses."

"The kids were babies," Jacobi said.

Brady shrugged. "The killer probably isn't using that kind of logic. As for the killing of the mothers, you're seeing a real hatred for women."

"In terms of finding this guy," Jacobi said, "his early childhood isn't relevant, is it? How he feels isn't going to lead us to him."

"You're right, Lieutenant. In fact, I'm going to say this guy can hide in plain sight. Look at what you know from the way he committed the crimes, how he got away without being seen. He's highly intelligent, he's focused, he's organized, and he's working alone. Most important, he passes as ordinary. That's the only way he could get so close to his victims. They don't even scream."

"And he's got a gun that doesn't bring up a hit," I said.

"That's an interesting detail," Brady said. "This guy knows weaponry. Makes me think he may have military training."

"We've got a witness ID and video sur-veillance," I said. "We think we have some idea what he may look like."

"Nothing distinctive, am I right?"

"Yeah," said Chi. "White male, thirties, wears a cap. We'll get another look when we go over the security tapes from One EC."

Conklin asked, "If this guy is military, if he's at least highly competent and trained, what's going to trip him up?"

"Overconfidence," Brady said. "He could get too sure of himself and leave a clue. But, you know, it could be a long time before he makes that kind of mistake."

I sat back in my seat. It was another way of saying what I'd been thinking since the Bentons were killed in the Stonestown garage.

More people were going to die.

Chapter 37

TEN DAYS AGO, "Dowling trumped everything."

Now the entire threadbare Homicide squad plus dozens of conscripted cops from other departments were canvassing the Embarcadero Center, following up every phoned-in, crackpot lead, working twelve-hour shifts under Jacobi in single-minded determination to nail the Lipstick Killer.

I was in the morgue with Claire when the ballistics report from the Feds was dropped into her in-box. I tried not to scream out my impatience as she carried on a phone call while gingerly peeling up the envelope flap. She finally hung up on her caller and took out the single sheet of paper. She skimmed the page and said,

"Hey-hey. Our case was reviewed by Dr. Mike himself."

"Forgive my ignorance—and will you please give me the damned report?"

"Hang on, girlfriend. Dr. Michael Sciarra is the FBI's Dr. Gun," she said. "Okay. Lemme get to the nub here. Dr. Mike says the gunpowder stippling on those dead babies was atypical because the shots were fired through a suppressor. And not your basic pop-bottle-and-scouring-pad wackadoo, either."

"What, then?" I asked.

"It had to be professionally tooled, cold steel or titanium. Very few of these exist. Dr. Mike says here, 'There is no record of any homicides in the United States committed with a suppressor like the one that caused the atypical stippling pattern on the Benton and Kinski children.'"

"Jeez, what the hell does that mean?"

"For starters, it explains why no one heard gunshots."

"And why we didn't get a hit in the database."

"Because it probably came from outside the country," Claire was saying when my cell phone buzzed. My stomach clenched when I read the caller ID. I showed the phone to Claire, flipped it open, and said, "Boxer."

I was thinking, *What now?*

"Boxer, that goddamned, shit-for-brains Lipstick Psycho put on another freakin' horror show!" Jacobi shouted into my ear.

"No, c'mon, NO."

"Yeah, well, a woman and child were killed in the parking garage at Union Square, looks exactly like the last two homicides. I'm at the scene with Chi and Cappy. Tracchio's on the way, and now he's going to put his mitts all over this."

I hung up with Jacobi, briefed Claire, and got Conklin on the line, then fled to the parking lot behind the Hall. Conklin was waiting for me in the driver's seat of our squad car, and as soon as I slammed my door closed, he jammed on the gas and we peeled out with flashers on, siren blaring, rubber burning tracks into the asphalt.

Conklin shouted over the clamor, "He does this smack in the middle of town. What a pair this guy has."

"Smack in the middle of town is what he likes. He's a terrorist. A damned good one."

I had no idea how right I would turn out to be.

Chapter 38

I SWEAR CONKLIN got the car up to three G's in three seconds. I gripped the dash as the Crown Vic roared up Leavenworth and then took us through the stomach-turning roller-coaster climbs, sudden-death drops, and hairpin turns of our city's streets.

When I wasn't mentally trying to steer the car from the passenger seat, I thought about the Lipstick Killer. He wasn't just insane.

He was *crazy*.

He'd killed four people—and now maybe more. His signature was so cryptic, it was meaningless. How could we predict his behavior if we didn't get his point?

Conklin wrenched the wheel right at the

bottom of a hill, sending us into a gridlocked intersection. I wanted to get out and beat on car roofs until the road was clear, but instead I shouted into the bullhorn, "Move your vehicles. Pull over now!"

We started and stopped as cars stalled trying to climb over one another, the seconds dragging until we cleared the jam. Minutes later, Conklin nosed the squad car between a small herd of parked black-and-whites outside the garage at Union Square. I was out of the car before Conklin set the brake.

Together we waded into the panicky throng of shoppers who had left their cars in the garage. I saw the fear on their faces and could almost hear their collective thoughts: *The killer was here. He could have shot me.*

I made a path through the crowd with my badge, signed the log, and asked Officer Sorbero to fill me in.

"Déjà vu all over again," Joe said. "The crime scene's on the fourth floor. We shut the elevators down."

Conklin held up the tape and we ducked under it, entering the chill of the garage. There were dark, tunneled access points on the ground floor, passageways coming from all sides—the huge Macy's, the Saks, the Sir Francis Drake Hotel—perfect opportunities for a predator to stalk his victims unseen.

As Conklin and I strode up the winding center double aisles between the rows of parked cars, I braced myself for what Jacobi had described as a "horror show." We found him talking with Chief Anthony Tracchio on the third-floor landing. The chief's face was blanched, and Jacobi's hooded eyes were drawn almost closed, both men looking as though they'd peered over the abyss into the devil's own lair.

"Chi and McNeil are on four," Tracchio said, his mouth hardly moving. "Swing shift is canvassing the perimeter. I've expanded the team to any cop who volunteers or who crosses my path."

"Were there any witnesses?" I asked. It was more a small, doomed wish than a question.

"No," Jacobi said. "No one saw or heard a fucking thing."

Chapter 39

CONKLIN AND I climbed past the angled rows of parked cars, my feelings of dread increasing the higher we went. By the time we greeted McNeil and Chi at the top of the fourth floor, I felt as if spiders were using the tops of my arms as a freeway, working their way under the hair at the back of my neck.

I didn't want to see the victims, yet I had to look. I forced my eyes down. And there, lying in an empty parking space between two vehicles, were the bodies.

The woman had been pretty, and she still retained grace in death. Her white sweater and long brunette hair were soaked with blood, which pooled around her and ran in long runnels down the sloping concrete floor. There were bloody footprints around her and blood on the bottoms of her shoes.

The child was tucked into the curl of the woman's body. It looked as though they had been posed.

My vision started to fade. I felt the ground shift under my feet and heard Conklin's voice. "Linds? Lindsay?" His arm around my waist stopped me from dropping to the floor.

"What's wrong? Are you okay?"

I nodded and mumbled, "I'm fine. Fine. I haven't eaten today." I was annoyed at myself for looking weak. For looking female. My superiors, the guys, my friends in the squad, would be looking to me for leadership. I had to get a grip.

The victims were bracketed between a red Dodge Caravan and a silver Highlander. An open handbag lay on the ground, and the contents of the victim's purse were scattered.

All of the Caravan's doors were open. I lifted my eyes to the windshield and saw the letters "CWF" written in red.

That strange signature again. What the hell did it mean?

Paul Chi called my name from behind my shoulder, and I turned to see his blanched face. I knew that, like me, Chi was shocked to the core by this terrible crime.

"The vic's name is Elaine Marone," Chi said. "Mrs. Marone was thirty-four. She had fifty-six dollars in her wallet, credit cards, a driver's license, and so on. We don't know the little girl's name."

"Did you find the lipstick?" I asked, hoping that it had rolled under a vehicle, that the killer had left a fingerprint on its shiny case.

"We found no makeup of any kind," Chi said. "But here's something new: check out the bruising on Mrs. Marone's wrist. Maybe she tried to disarm the shooter."

I crouched next to the body of Elaine Marone. As Chi said, there were bluish finger marks on the woman's right wrist, and I counted five distinct bullet holes in her sweater. Elaine Marone hadn't just put up a struggle. She'd fought like hell.

And then the screaming started, a heartrending howl twisting up through the concrete cavern.

"Laineeee. Lilllly."

Oh God, no.

Footsteps pounded on concrete. Jacobi yelled, "Stop! Freeze right where you are!"

It was a clear warning, but the footsteps kept coming.

Chapter 40

I RAN DOWN the incline toward the third floor, then rounded the turn to see Tracchio and Jacobi tackling a big man wearing jeans and a flannel shirt. The man was a bruiser, a charging bull on full adrenaline. He shook off Tracchio and Jacobi as if they were small dogs, then continued running up the ramp toward the crime scene. It looked like he was going to blast right through me.

Jacobi yelled, "FREEZE," then pulled his Taser from his belt. I shouted, "Jacobi, NO! Don't do it, don't—" But I knew he had no choice. I heard the electric chattering of the stun gun, and the big man was jerked off his feet, going down as if his spinal cord had been cut. He flopped and slid down the incline, a five-second ride, and during that time he was paralyzed and unable to scream.

Jacobi caught up to him, shouting, "Jesus Christ, look what you made me do! Are you done now? Are you done?"

The rattle of the Taser stopped and the fallen man's horrific sobbing began—and he couldn't stop. I stooped beside him as Jacobi twisted back his arms and snapped on the cuffs.

"I'm Sergeant Boxer," I said, patting the man down. I lifted his wallet from his back pocket and checked his face against his driver's license photo. The man was Francis Marone.

"Let me UP. I have to go to them!"

I said, "I'm sorry, Mr. Marone, not right now."

"What happened? Are they okay?" Marone choked out. "I just spoke to Elaine." He sobbed. "I had to stop for cigarettes, but I told her I'd meet her at the car."

"You were talking to her on the phone just now?"

"I heard her say to someone, 'What do you want?' And then I heard—oh God, tell me she's okay."

I said again that I was sorry as Marone cried, "NO, not my girls. Please, please, I have to go to them."

Francis Marone was breaking my heart—and this was the savage part: if we ever expected to catch, let alone indict, the killer, we had to protect the crime scene from this man.

A forest of legs had grown up around me—Tracchio, Conklin, Chi, McNeil. I asked Mr. Marone if there was a friend or relative I could call for him, but he wasn't listening. Still, I had to know: "Mr. Marone, can you think of anyone who may have wanted to harm your wife?"

Marone searched my face with his bloodshot eyes before shouting, "I operate a cement mixer! Elaine does PR for a toy store! We're nobodies. *Nobodies*."

Marone was bleeding from bad scrapes on his forearms. I put my hand on the poor guy's shoulder and stood aside as Jacobi and Tracchio got him to his feet.

"I didn't want to hurt you, man," Jacobi said.

I signaled to officers Noonan and Mackey, asking them to drive Marone to the hospital. I promised Marone I'd meet him there as soon as I could. Then I got out of the way as Claire's van tore up the ramp.

Chapter 41

CLAIRE WAS STOWING her camera by the time I made it back up to the fourth tier. She looked into my face, and I saw my own horror reflected in hers. We opened our arms and held on to each other, and this time I didn't care who thought I was weak.

"These babies. I can't take the babies," I said.

"It's *not* going to be all right," Claire said into my shoulder. "Even when you catch the bastard, it's *not* going to be all right. Not ever again. You know that, right?"

We broke apart as one of Claire's assistants asked her if it was okay to start bagging the victims' hands. The grim work of deconstructing the crime had begun. I said to Claire,

"Did you see the letters on the windshield?"

"Uh-huh. CWF. That's another kink in the pattern. The 'C' and the 'W' are still next to each other, so the 'F' is moving around. And that's all I've got except for two more DBs to work up who shouldn't be dead."

Claire pulled at my arm, and I stepped out of the way as Clapper's crime scene–mobile steamed up the rise and stopped beside the ME's van. CSIs poured out of the back, and Clapper stood over the sickening tableau and said to no one in particular, "Makes you wonder if the Good Lord has just given up on humanity."

Cameras flashed and video was shot of the bodies and of the bullet dings in the car both inside and out. Slugs were collected for evidence. Markers were set out, sketches were drawn, and notes were taken.

I stood aside and watched the CSIs work, thinking about how an hour before, Elaine Marone had been shopping with her husband and her toddler, and now Claire's team was wrapping their bodies in clean white sheets, zipping up the body bags. I was glad the cold finality of those zippers closing was something

Francis Marone would never hear.

I was wishing again, hoping that the spent slugs would compute, that there would be some useful physical evidence in this bloodbath, when Conklin called out, "Linds. Check this out."

I walked over to the Marones' minivan and saw that my partner was pointing to the three-letter signature on the windshield. He turned his brown eyes on me and said, "That's not lipstick."

I shined my light on the letters and felt my stomach drop.

"That's blood," Conklin said. "He wrote the letters in their blood with his finger."

One of Clapper's techs took close-ups. Another swabbed the letters on the windshield. My flicker of hope burned bright.

Could it be?

Had the Lipstick Killer gotten so lost in his madness, he'd left a bloody print behind for the good guys?

Chapter 42

AT EIGHT THIRTY that night, Sergeant Jackson Brady faced the motley gang of Homicide inspectors and patrol cops who were grouped around him in our squad room. He jammed a videotape into our old machine and said, "If anyone sees something I missed, shout it out."

The screen sparked with a grainy black-and-white image of a man in the lower right corner, walking up the center aisle of the garage, heading toward the Dodge Caravan near the end of the row.

The images were halting, dark, snowy—the result of bad lighting and cheap tape that had been recycled hundreds of times. Still, we could see the killer. As before, he wore a billed cap and a two-toned baseball jacket. He kept his head down and faced away from the surveillance camera.

Brady narrated as the pictures rolled.

"Here, he has his hands in his pockets. As he approaches the victim's van, he hails Mrs. Marone. What's he saying? Asking the time, maybe? Or does she have change for a twenty?

"Now she puts her packages on the van's backseat and slides the door closed. She goes to the driver's side, talking on the cell phone to her husband."

I watched the screen as the killer moved in on the still-living figure of Elaine Marone. I studied the way he walked, examining his body language and hers. He seemed apologetic as he went toward her, and Elaine Marone didn't appear alarmed.

I remembered Brady saying that this guy "passes as ordinary." And I thought about the most vicious of the serial killers—the ones that movies were made about—and every one of those psychopaths looked ordinary.

"See, now, the gun is out," Brady said. "Nine mil, Beretta. Nifty suppressor. She takes a quick look into the backseat, then stretches out the handbag. She's saying, 'What do you want?' She's trying to buy the killer off, not getting anywhere. The Highlander blocks the camera's view of their lower bodies, but from the way he's suddenly bent over, I think she's kicked him.

"Now he's slapping the handbag out of her hand, and there's the first gunshot. She presses her hand to her upper chest."

Brady talked, but I could see for myself that Elaine Marone went for the killer's gun hand. He grabbed her wrist with his free hand, squeezing it hard, and he wrenched himself free. That's when he left bruises on her wrist. A second later, Elaine Marone's body jerked four times, then slumped out of sight.

The back door of the van was opened, and the killer fired one shot into the backseat, then disappeared from view.

"Look," Brady said. "Here's our shooter again. He's holding Elaine Marone's body around the waist with his left arm and using the index finger of her right hand to write his signature on the glass. She didn't have lipstick," Brady said, "so he improvised."

I asked Brady to roll the tape back, and I watched again as the killer used the dead woman's hand to write "CWF" in her blood. He used *her* finger, not his, and besides, the bastard was wearing gloves. My hope for a fingerprint died.

Brady was saying, "He left the van doors open and arranged the bodies. Now here he is, walking up toward the fifth tier, where the next camera picks him up getting into the elevator. We have the tape from that, too. It's ten seconds, a close-up of the top of his cap, no logo. Now he exits at street level.

"Three minutes and forty seconds," Brady said, pointing the remote at the monitor, shutting it off. "That's how much time elapsed from when he drew his gun to when he disappeared."

Chapter 43

WE WERE ON the wide leather couch in the living room, waiting for the eleven o'clock news. My feet were in Joe's lap, and Martha was snoring on the rug beside me. I was frustrated and beyond exhaustion. I wanted to sleep, but my mind was spinning.

"A woman came into the Hall today," I said to Joe. "She told Jacobi that a man approached her outside the Ferry Building the night the Kinskis were killed. Said he was lost. He was wearing a billed cap and a blue-and-white baseball jacket."

"She was credible?"

"Jacobi said she was shaking and had half chewed her lip off. She told Jacobi the guy was creepy. She said she couldn't help him and walked away with her baby, and he shouted after her, 'I appreciate the fucking time of day!' She's seen the surveillance video and thinks it could be him."

"Good news, Linds. A witness, of sorts."

"It's something, but, you know, it could have been anyone wearing a baseball jacket. Joe, WCF, FWC. And now CWF. You're a puzzle addict. What do you get out of that?"

"West Coast Freak. Factory Workers' Coalition. Chief Wacko Freak. Want me to keep going?"

"No, you're right," I said. "It's gooseberries. The shooter is playing with us."

"Listen, before I forget to tell you—"

"There," I said, grabbing the clicker off the coffee table, amping up the volume as the familiar face of news anchor Andrea Costella talked above the "Breaking News" banner.

"We have news tonight about the Lipstick Killer, who was videotaped at a Union Square garage as he was leaving the scene of another horrific double homicide," she said.

The video came on the screen, about ten seconds of the shooter entering the elevator car, stabbing the button with a gloved hand, and standing in one place, eyes lowered, until the doors opened and he exited into thin air.

"An anonymous witness described the shooter to the police, who have made a sketch available to this station," Costella said. A drawing replaced the videotape on the screen.

"See?" I said to Joe. "Mr. Ordinary. No-color eyes, no-color hair. Regular features, regular nine mil slugs, no match to anything. But not mentioned to the viewers, he uses a suppressor, professional grade."

"Sounds like he's military. Special Ops. Or he's a military contractor. Got the suppressor on the black market or overseas."

"Yeah. The military angle makes sense. But there are, what, thousands and thousands of former military guys in the city? And half of them fit this guy's description. Hey, what's this?" I asked as another video came on the screen.

I watched with my mouth open as a handheld camera bumped along behind Claire. It was recording her leaving the morgue, heading to the parking lot just outside her office. Reporters fired questions about the victims and asked her if there was anything she could tell the people of San Francisco.

Claire turned her back to the cameras and got into her new Prius. She started it up, and I thought that was it—*Get lost, you vultures*—but she buzzed down the window, rested her elbow on the frame, and looked squarely at the cameras.

"Yes, I have something to tell the people of San Francisco, and I'm not speaking as the chief medical examiner. I'm speaking as a wife and a mother. Are we clear?"

There was a chorus of yeses.

"Moms, keep your eyes open," Claire said. "Don't trust anyone. Don't park in lonely places, and don't get near your car unless there are other people around. And, no kidding, get a license to carry a handgun. Then *carry* it."

Chapter 44

PETE GORDON SAT in the kitchen, laptop in front of him on the red Formica table, his back to the porch where Sherry was doing stupid puppet tricks for her brother. The stink bomb was shrieking with joy or fright, Pete really didn't know which, because it was all like having a screwdriver jabbed through his eardrum.

Pete yelled over his shoulder, "Keep it down, Sherry! In a minute, I'm going to take off my belt."

"We'll be quiet, Daddy."

Gordon returned to the letter he was composing, a kind of ransom note. Yeah. He liked thinking of it that way. He was a pretty good writer, but this had to be crystal clear and without any clues to his identity.

"An open letter to the citizens of San Francisco," he wrote. "I have something important to tell you."

He thought about the word "citizens," decided it was too stiff, and replaced it with "residents." Much better.

"An open letter to the residents of San Francisco." Then he changed the second line: "I have a proposition to make." Suddenly there was a shrill scream from the porch, and Sherry was shushing the stink bomb and then calling in through the window, "Daddy, I'm sorry, please don't get mad. Stevie didn't mean it."

The baby was crying on both the inhale and the exhale, un-fucking-relenting. Pete clenched his hands, thinking how much he hated them and everything about the life he lived now. *Look at me, Ladies and Gentlemen, Captain Peter Gordon, former commando, currently Househusband First Class.*

What a frickin' tragedy.

The only thing that gave him joy anymore was working on his plan. Thinking how, after he'd wasted Sherry and the stink bomb, it was going to give him great, great pleasure to show the princess who he really was. He could hardly wait to silence her nagging. *Pete, sweetie, don't forget to pick up the milk and don't forget to take your meds, okay? Hey, handsome, did you make lunch for the kids? Make the bed? Call the cable guy?*

He imagined Heidi's face, pale in the middle of all that red hair, eyes like yo-yos when she realized what he had done. And what he was going to do to her.

Hi-hi, Heidi. Bye-dee-bye.

WOMEN'S MURDER CLUB

Part Three

THE TRAP

Chapter 45

SARAH WELLS CROUCHED in the shrubbery between the huge Tudor-style house and the street, her clothes blending into the shadows. She was having a three-dimensional flashback of the Dowling job—how she'd hidden in the closet while the Dowlings made love, later knocking into that table of whatnots during her narrow frickin' escape. And then the worst part—the murder accusation hanging over her.

She considered quitting while she was ahead. On the other hand, the Morley house was a prize.

The three-story white home with dark beams and bay windows belonged to Jim and Dorian Morley, the Sports Gear Morleys who owned a chain of athletic stores up and down the coast.

She'd read everything about them on the Web and seen dozens of photos. Dorian Morley dressed to impress and owned a stunning jewelry collection that she kept in constant use.

Sarah had made special note of Mrs. Morley telling a *Chronicle* reporter that she loved to wear diamonds every day, "even around the house."

Imagine. Everyday diamonds.

Which is why Sarah had put the Morleys on her to-do list, done several run-throughs to check out the traffic patterns at nine p.m. in their neighborhood, and pinpointed where to stash her car and where to hide. On one of her drive-bys earlier in the week, she'd even seen Jim Morley leaving the house in his Mercedes. He was stocky and muscular — the kind of build people called "brawny."

Sarah definitely did not want to run into Jim Morley tonight. And she wouldn't. The Morleys were having a *Big Chill* party in their backyard and would be treating their friends to a live performance of a retread rock-and-roll band from the '60s. She could hear the first set now, electric guitars twanging over screeching mics.

What a fantastic cover of sound.

Fifteen minutes ago, one of the valets had parked the last guest's car down the hill and was now hanging out in the street with his buddy. Sarah could hear their muted laughter and smell the cigarette smoke.

She was going to do it. She'd made up her mind. And there was *no better time than now*.

Sarah glanced up at the Morleys' bedroom window, and, after taking a breath, she darted out from the sheltering shrubbery and ran twenty feet to the base of the house. Once there, she executed a maneuver like the one she'd practiced many times on the climbing wall at the gym. She jammed the left toe of her climbing shoe against the clapboard, gripped the drainpipe of the gutter with her right hand, and stretched up to the window ledge.

Halfway through the ten-foot climb, her left foot slipped, and she hung, heart pounding, body splayed vertically against the wall, right hand gripping the drainpipe, desperate not to pull down the gutter and create a clamor that would end with a shout or a rough hand at her back.

Quit now, Sarah. Go home.

Sarah hung against the wall for interminable seconds.

Her forearms were like cables from hours of just hanging by her hands from the bar across her closet doorway—not just until she couldn't hold on for another instant but until her muscles failed and she peeled off the bar. She'd strengthened her fingers by squeezing a rubber ball when she drove her car, watched TV—any spare moment at all. But despite her strength and determination, there was still some light from the moon, and Sarah Wells was not invisible.

As she clung to the wall, Sarah heard a car stop around the corner of the house and voices of new guests coming up the walk. She waited for them to enter the house, and when she figured it was safe, she took her hand off the drainpipe and reached for the molding below the window. When she had a firm grip, she pulled herself up until she was able to hook a leg onto the sill of the westernmost window of the Morleys' bedroom.

She was in.

Chapter 46

SARAH WRIGGLED OVER the sill and dropped to the carpet.

Her head swam with a high-octane blend of elation, urgency, and fear. She glanced at the digital clock on the nightstand beside the Morleys' huge four-poster bed and registered the time. It was 9:14, and Sarah swore to herself that once the blue digits read 9:17, she'd be gone.

The spacious room was dimly lit from the light in the hall. Sarah took in the heavy, Queen Anne–period maple furnishings, evidence of an inheritance as well as the bazillions the Morleys had made in sporting goods. There were little oil paintings near the bed, a huge plasma-screen TV in the armoire, photos along the walls of the handsome Morley clan in sailboats—walls that now thrummed with a pounding rock-and-roll beat.

Sarah was on her mark and ready to go. She crossed the long, carpeted room, then shut the door leading out to the hallway and locked it. Now, except for the blinking blue light of the digital clock, she was completely in the dark.

It was 9:15.

Sarah felt along the wall, found the closet door, opened it, and threw on the switch to her headlamp. The room-sized closet was fantastic, and she wouldn't have expected less from the Morleys. There were racks and racks of clothes, hers on one side, his on the other; a triple-paned floor-to-ceiling mirror at the back wall; everything you could ever ask from a closet—except a safe. Where was it?

Sarah worked quickly, looking behind evening gowns and running her fingers along baseboard moldings and shelves, feeling time whiz by as she inventoried the Morleys' frickin' closet.

She would have to leave. Empty-handed.

Sarah had just turned off her light and exited the closet when she heard footsteps on the hardwood. They stopped outside the bedroom. The doorknob twisted back and forth, then a man's voice shouted, "Hey! Who locked the door?"

Sarah froze. Should she hide? Break for the window in the dark?

The man called out again: "It's Jim. I need to use the can." His laugh was sloppy with drink. He put on a high-pitched, fruity voice. "Hello Kitty? Is that youuuu?"

Sarah's heart nearly stopped. It was Jim Morley, and he was pounding on his bedroom door.

"Hey. Open up!"

Chapter 47

SARAH RAN TO the window, whatever might be in her way be damned. She had her hand on the sill when a door opened into the room and light poured in. Morley had entered the bathroom from the room next door, and his hulking frame was silhouetted by the bathroom light.

He called out as he fumbled for the switch on the bedroom wall. "Is someone here?"

Sarah's mind did a backflip. Without the light, she could see him better than he could see her. She had to brazen it out. "Jim," she said, "can you give us some privacy, please?"

"Laura? Laura, is that you? Jesus. I'm sorry. You and Jesse, take your time. Take all the time you need."

The bathroom door closed. The darkness returned. *Take all the time you need,* Morley had said, but when he got back to the party, he'd see Laura and Jesse, and he'd sound the alarm.

It was 9:20.

Sarah had a foot up on the sill when an image appeared in the corner of her mind's eye. She'd been in a rush to get to the closet, but she'd half noticed a particular painting of a wheat field right next to the bed. Had it been hinged to the wall?

Thirty seconds, no more, but she had to check it out.

Sarah found the four-poster by the pale blue light of the clock and used it to guide her. Her fingers ran across the edges of the small picture frame, and then she pulled it toward her.

She exhaled as the painting swung open. Behind it was a cool metal box with its padlock hanging open. Sarah moved quickly. She pulled the box from the wall, set it down on the bed, and flipped back the lid. Then she opened the empty duffel bag she'd brought for the loot and began to transfer small bulging envelopes and boxes out of the safe.

When her bag was full, she zipped it closed and

returned the empty box to its sleeve in the wall.

Time to go!

Sarah peered out the window and saw a man walking his rottie. He stopped to talk to the valet, then continued up the street. Sarah vaulted onto the sill and turned so that she faced into the room. She placed her hands on the ledge between her bent legs and then let herself down and over the side. She jammed her climbing shoes against the wall of the house, then dropped.

Her foot hit a hollow in the lawn, and her ankle turned.

She stifled a yelp, clenching her teeth in a grimace. Then, hidden by clouds crossing the moon, Sarah hobbled through the dark toward her car.

Chapter 48

SARAH ALMOST CRIED out in relief when she saw her red Saturn parked along the street not far from the Morleys' house. She got inside, whipped off her lamp and knit hat in one movement, and stripped off her gloves. She stuffed them into the duffel with the jewelry cases and slid the bag under the front seat.

She sat in the comforting dark of night, gripping the steering wheel, her ankle throbbing as she marveled at her minutes-long, heart-stopping escapade.

It was unbelievable.

Jim Morley had called her "Hello Kitty."

He'd opened the bathroom door and stared right at her. And still she hadn't gotten caught.

Hadn't gotten caught *yet,* Sarah reminded herself. She was carrying enough evidence under her car seat to get her locked up for twenty years, and that's if she wasn't charged with murder.

Sarah fluffed up her hair, slipped on the blue quilted shirt she kept in the backseat, and started up the engine. She rolled out onto Columbus, carefully keeping to the speed limit as she headed toward Bay Street, passing Chestnut and Francisco, her mind floating on the aftermath of her success, starting to think now about seeing Heidi.

She imagined telling Heidi the truth about herself, about how the loot she'd stolen would fund their freedom for maybe the rest of their lives, how their fantasies of living together as a family would come true.

As she thought about Heidi clapping her hands and throwing her arms around her, a distant sound nagged at Sarah until she couldn't ignore the whine any longer. The looping, high-pitched wail came from behind, getting louder as it approached. She could see red flashers in her rearview mirror.

Cops.

They couldn't be coming for her, could they? Had Jim Morley called the police after all? Maybe the valet had seen her limping down the street when Morley sounded the alarm. Still, she was sure no one had followed her to the car.

How had she screwed up?

Sarah's mind churned and her heart nearly pounded out of her chest as she pulled over to the side of the road. She pushed the duffel bag even farther under the seat, and then, keeping her eyes on the rearview mirror, Sarah Wells watched as the police cruiser pulled up behind her and braked.

Chapter 49

IN THE MOMENTS Sarah needed to construct an alibi, her mind foundered. She was far from her own neighborhood, and she was sure she looked guilty of something. Her whole body filmed over with sweat as the cruiser door opened and the man with the brimmed hat stepped out and walked toward her.

His eyes were shadowed by his hat, but Sarah took in the square jaw, the straight nose, the unsmiling mouth. He looked every bit like an official with no slack to cut.

"License and registration, please."

"Yes, sir," Sarah said, fumbling in the glove box, finding her wallet on top of the maps, hands slippery from nerves, credit cards shooting out of her fingers and onto the floor. Sarah picked up her driver's license, dove back into the glove box to retrieve the registration card, and handed one after the other to the officer.

"Sir, did I do something wrong? Was I speeding?"

The officer shined his light on the documents and, saying he'd be back in a moment, returned to his car to run her name through the computer.

Cherry lights flashed in her mirror. Sarah's only cogent thought was that the Morley burglary was the stupidest thing she'd ever done. She imagined the officer ordering her out of the car, telling her to put her hands on the hood. She saw how easily he would find Dorian Morley's jewelry.

As time dragged on, she imagined other police cars coming, cops surrounding her, laughing at how she'd been caught red-handed. She imagined the interrogation that would go on until she confessed—which would be immediately, because there would be no explaining away the evidence.

The pain in Sarah's ankle was excruciating, and along with it was a swooping dizziness that turned to nausea.

What would happen to her? What would happen to Heidi?

A beam hit her eyes; the officer had returned, one hand holding the flashlight, the other handing back her documentation.

"Your left taillight is busted," he said. "You need to get that fixed right way."

Sarah apologized, sounding ridiculously guilty to her own ears, saying she hadn't realized the light was broken, promising she'd go to the auto shop—and then it was over. As the cruiser sailed past her, Sarah opened the car door and vomited into the street. Then she rested her forehead against the steering wheel.

"Thank you, God," she said out loud.

Her hands were still shaking as she started up the car again and headed to Marina Boulevard. Skimming along the street, she turned her eyes to the Golden Gate Bridge, the chains of lights blazing. It was a sign, that necklace of lights, and Sarah's optimism was reborn, this time as euphoria.

She hadn't made any costly mistakes. She'd done her homework on the Morleys and had pulled off a first-class heist that brought her that much closer to her goal. And now she had a brilliant idea.

Along with getting her taillight fixed as soon as possible, she was going to call Maury Green's widow. She'd make Mrs. Green an offer, a finder's fee if she'd hook Sarah up with another fence.

And more thoughts came flooding in, those envelopes full of Dorian Morley's everyday diamonds. She couldn't wait to see what else she'd taken from the safe.

Chapter 50

SARAH OPENED THE door to the one-bedroom apartment she shared with her revolting, hair-trigger husband. She stood listening for a moment in the small foyer, and when she heard snoring, she stepped into the living room. "Terror" was slumped in his brown leather recliner, asleep in his wife beater and shorts, his plaid underwear not only showing but unsnapped and open.

She wrinkled her nose at the porn couple silently humping on the TV, then slipped past her husband and into the bedroom, where she closed the door and quietly threw the lock.

Only then did she feel that it was safe to draw a real breath. She jerked the curtains closed and flicked on the overhead light. Then she opened her duffel bag full of loot and spilled the bulging envelopes onto the bedspread.

Sarah's breathing was shallow and her eyes were bright as she unsnapped each little packet and liberated the contents. Diamond necklaces spilled out like streams of faceted ice. She touched each of the jewel-encrusted bracelets and brooches and pendants and rings with the tips of her fingers, stunned by her audacity and at the same time mesmerized by each splendid work of art.

Dorian Morley's taste was wonderful. The diamond necklaces were new but the packets of finely worked antiques seemed to be part of a personal collection. And so Sarah wondered if this treasure had been inherited or collected piece by piece by Dorian Morley herself.

And for the first time since she'd started stealing from the rich, Sarah knew that the woman who had owned these jewels was going to be grief-stricken when she discovered the loss.

This was not a good thought for a jewel thief, so she scrubbed it from her mind, reminding herself that the Morleys of this world had insurance and means, while she and Heidi had no fallback, no rescuers but themselves, and that each day they lived with their husbands was one of loathing and terrible risk.

Sarah returned the pieces to their packets and opened the bottom drawer of her dresser. She pushed the T-shirts and sweatpants aside, lifted the thin board of the false bottom, and deposited the tool bag.

Before she stowed the Morley jewels, Sarah had to see *it* one more time. She reached into the back right corner of the secret stash and felt for the little leather box shaped like a round-topped trunk.

The box fit perfectly in her closed hand. She opened the lid and stared at Casey Dowling's wonderful ring. It glittered under the light as if it were alive.

That yellow stone. Wow. It was *magnificent*.

Chapter 51

CONKLIN MUTTERED TO me as he parked the squad car in front of the Tudor-style mansion on Russian Hill.

"What a coincidence, huh? Hello Kitty does a job the same night the Lipstick Killer attacks Elaine Marone and her child."

"Rich, when my eyes flash open, you know? After three hours of sleep, I think it's all too much, that the Job is getting to me, that I should quit before it kills me. And then I ask myself what the hell I would do after that."

"When I get those thoughts, I think of opening a scuba shop in Martinique."

"Well, be nice to the Morleys. They can probably help you out with that."

Conklin stifled his laugh as the massive front door opened. Dorian Morley was tall, about forty, an attractive woman in a flowered tunic and black pants, her brown hair twisted up and pinned with a clip. She was also red-eyed and looked shaken. She invited us into the kitchen—a vast, well-lit space with sea-green glass counters and stainless-steel everything else. Her husband was sitting at the table with a mug of coffee in his large hand. He stood as she introduced us.

"I feel like an ass," Jim Morley said when we'd taken seats at the table. "The bedroom door was locked. That was weird. I said, 'Hello Killy? Is that youuuu?'" He made a gagging noise and shook his head. "Why is it you never think it could happen to you?"

Morley went on to say that he'd gone through the guest room and gotten into the bathroom that way.

"You saw the burglar?" I asked, hoping against disbelief.

"Nah, the lights were out in the bedroom," Morley said. "She pleaded with me, asked me to give her some privacy, and that's what convinced me it was a friend of ours, Laura Chenoweth. She and her husband, Jesse, are going through a rough patch, and I thought they were making up, you know, in private.

"Anyway, the newspapers keep referring to Hello Kitty as a man, right?"

I was reeling from this new information.

If Hello Kitty was a woman, it was our first real lead. A blind lead to be sure, but something!

"I just tossed the jewelry from the party on top of the dresser," Dorian Morley said. "I didn't even know we'd been robbed until I went to put my jewels in the safe."

She lowered her head into her hands and began to cry softly. Her husband said to us, "A lot of the jewelry belonged to Dorian's mom. Some of it was her grandmother's. What are the chances of getting it back?"

I was still stuck on the idea that our cat burglar was a woman. I heard Conklin say that so far none of the stolen goods had surfaced from the previous Hello Kitty burglaries, and then Dorian Morley lifted her head and said, "It's not just about the jewelry, Jim. It's about the fact that a murderer was inside our house. Inside our bedroom.

"What if you had challenged her instead of walking away? My God, Jim, she could have shot you!"

Chapter 52

BEING SUMMONED TO Tracchio's office is always an adventure. You never know if you're going to get a high five or a front-row seat on a meltdown.

Tracchio hung up the phone as Jacobi, Chi, and I took seats around the curve of his mahogany desk and watched him pat his comb-over. I don't dislike Tracchio, but I never forget that he's a bureaucrat doing a job only a real cop should do.

"The mayor has me on his speed dial," he was saying as his assistant brought him a fresh cup of tea. "I'm in his 'favorites' list, you understand, one of the top five. This morning, I made it to number one—when he saw this."

Tracchio flashed the morning's *Chronicle* with its photo of Claire leaning out her car window under the headline "Get a Gun."

I flushed, both scared and embarrassed for my best friend.

"One of our own said this," Tracchio said, his voice rising. "Told our citizens to carry guns, and the mayor says that all of us, and that includes you, you, and especially you," he said, stabbing a pudgy finger at Jacobi, "don't know your ass from a lemon tart."

Jacobi half rose to his feet in defense, but Tracchio put out a hand to silence and seat him.

"Don't say anything, Jacobi. I'm not in the mood. And I've got something else to show you."

Tracchio opened a folder on his desk, took out a sheet of newsprint, turned it around, and pushed it toward us. "This is going to run in tomorrow morning's *Chronicle*. The publisher sent an advance copy out to the mayor, who passed it around."

I read the headline: "An Open Letter to the Residents of San Francisco." Tracchio leaned back and said, "Go on, Boxer. Read that out loud."

"'An open letter to the residents of San Francisco,'" I read obediently. "'I have a proposition to make. It's very simple. I want two million dollars in cash and a contact person I can trust. Once I have the money, I will leave San Francisco for good and the killings of the women and children will stop. I expect a published reply and then we'll work out the details. Have a nice day.' It's not signed, but I guess we know who wrote this."

My head throbbed at the idea of it.

"Sir, you're not really thinking we're going to pay off the Lipstick Killer?" I asked Tracchio.

"Not out of our budget, of course, but a private citizen has already stepped forward with the cash, yes."

"Chief, we can't let anyone pay off a murderer. It opens the way for every freak with a gun and a sick idea—"

"She's right," Jacobi said. "You know that, Tony. Giving in to him is the worst thing we can do."

Tracchio leaned forward, smacked the flat of his hand down on the newsprint, and said, "You all listen to me. Several innocent people have been shot dead in the last couple of weeks. Forty men and women are working this case around the clock, and we've got nothing. Nothing. Except the chief medical examiner saying that people should start packing.

"What choice do I have? None. This letter is going to run," the chief said, glaring at each of us in turn, "and I can't stop it. So figure out how to catch this psycho. Set a trap. How you do it is up to you. I know it's hard. That's why it's called 'work.' Now, I need my office. I've got to call the mayor."

Chapter 53

I JOGGED BACK down the stairs with Chi and Jacobi, the three of us wrapped in our own mortified silence. Yes, Tracchio's drubbing was humiliating, but far worse was the fact that the city was being held hostage by a psychopath. And Tracchio was in such a bind, he was giving in to a terrorist.

Apparently the giving-in was already in motion. Someone in the mayor's inner circle had stepped forward with two million dollars to pay off the Lipstick Killer before his letter even ran. It was insane, completely magical thinking to believe that if we handed the killer his millions, he would leave town. And even if he did, where would he go? What would he do when he got there? And how many more crazies would be inspired to commit murder for pay?

When Jacobi, Chi, and I walked into the squad room, all eyes turned to us, the silent question hanging in the air like a thundercloud.

What did the chief say?

Jacobi stopped at the head of the room. He was livid, biting off each word as he said to the six men staring up at him, "The Lipstick Killer wants two million bucks to stop the killings. The chief wants us to set a trap."

The gasping and commentary were as loud as that thundercloud breaking into a downpour. "That's enough," Jacobi said. "Boxer's in charge. Sergeant, keep me posted. Every hour. On the hour."

I sat down at my desk across from Conklin, and Chi dragged up a chair. I filled Conklin in on the beat-down we'd taken from Tracchio as I dialed Henry Tyler. I was passed from automatic menu to Tyler's personal assistant, then to Muzak as I was put on hold.

Henry Tyler is a powerful man, the associate publisher of the *San Francisco Chronicle*. His daughter, Madison, had been kidnapped a while ago, a sweet, precocious little girl, some kind of musical prodigy.

Because of Conklin's work and mine, Madison Tyler had *not* been found dead in a ditch. Instead, she was playing the piano, going to school, and romping with her little dog.

Tyler and his wife had been so grateful to Conklin and me for saving Madison's life, Tyler had said he owed us a big favor. I hoped he'd remember that promise—and then he was on the line.

Chapter 54

"MR. TYLER," I said into the phone, calling up a mental image of the tall, gray-haired man. The last time I'd seen him, he'd been in the park with his little girl. He'd been laughing.

"Lindsay, I've told you, call me Henry," Tyler said now. "I've been expecting your call. It's too bad it has to be about this guy."

"We're glad he's surfaced," I told Tyler. "It's an opportunity, but only if we have time to work up a plan. Can you stall him, Henry? What if you don't run his letter tomorrow, maybe give us another day?"

"How can I do that? If I don't run his letter and he kills more people, it'll be my fault—and I can't live with that. But, Lindsay, I can get the money for him. I was hoping you could be our go-between."

"You're paying him the two million?"

"It's cheap any way you look at it," Tyler said to me. "He could have asked five times as much, and paying him off would still be the right thing to do. He's going to keep killing kids and their mothers unless we give him what he wants—you know that. I'm sure that he's had this payout in mind from the beginning."

I was startled to hear Henry Tyler say he was going to pay off the killer and even more stunned at his conclusion: that the Lipstick Killer's spree had been about the money all along.

"Henry, what worries me is that buying off the killer won't stop him from killing, and it will only encourage others to make similar threats."

"I understand, Lindsay. We have to trip him up somehow. That's why I'll be working with you."

My headache had gone molten right between my eyes. I was a cop, nothing more. I couldn't see through walls or into the mind of a psycho. While it was flattering that Henry Tyler thought I could stop the Lipstick Killer, it was obvious the murderer was smart—too smart to fall for your basic van full of cops waiting for him to pick up a briefcase of money.

The worst-case scenario was the one that seemed the most likely: Killer gets the cash. Killer gets away. Killer continues to kill. And he inspires terrorism all over the country. There weren't enough cops in America to cover an epidemic of sickos killing for money.

"I want to be sure I understand," I said to Tyler. "You haven't been in touch with the Lipstick Killer. He doesn't know you're going to give him the money?"

"He doesn't know about me at all. He's paid for us to run the letter, and he'll be waiting for a response by way of a return letter in the paper. I can stall, get the money, and write a reply to run the day after tomorrow."

"So we have two days."

"Yes. I guess that's right."

"You've got a new secretary starting tomorrow morning," I said to Tyler. "I'll be with you round the clock."

Chapter 55

THERE WAS A pile of doughnuts in the coffee room, and I went for them. I hadn't eaten a square meal in almost two weeks, and hadn't had more than five consecutive hours of sleep in that time, either. As for exercise, zero, unless my brain running 24-7 on a hamster wheel counted for something.

I sugared my coffee, went back into the squad room, and saw Cindy sitting at my seat, smiling over the desk at Conklin and shaking her bouncy blond curls.

"Linds," she said, getting up to give me a hug.

"Hey, Cindy," I said, hugging her a little too tightly, "Rich and I have something to tell you—off the record."

"That Hello Kitty is female?"

I glared at my partner, who shrugged at me.

"That's not for publication," I said, swinging down into my seat, watching Cindy pull up a chair. I piled my doughnuts on a paper napkin and placed my coffee cup on a file folder.

"I had put together this whole list of social-register guys who could climb up the side of a house," Cindy said, pulling a sheet from her computer case. "Duke Edgerton, William Burke Ruffalo, and Peter Carothers are rock climbers. They were on top of my all-star list, but now they're the wrong gender, right? Since Kitty's a girl."

"We have no idea if the woman in the Morleys' house was Hello Kitty or a party guest Jim Morley didn't know," I said to Cindy, "so let's not get crazy and print that, okay?"

"Hmmmm."

"Cindy, we will not be able to vet a single lead that comes in if you print that Hello Kitty is female."

"The Morleys had fifty guests last night," Cindy said. "You think the word's not going to get out?"

"There's a difference between rumor and a

police confirmation," I said. "But you already know that."

Cindy sniffed. "What if I say, 'Sources close to the police department have confirmed to the *Chronicle* that they have new information that could lead to the identity of the cat burglar known as Hello Kitty'?"

"Okay," I said. "Write that. Now just in case your boss didn't already tell you—"

"Henry? Oh, he did. What a scorcher, huh? A letter from the Lipstick Killer going into the front section."

"Well, you're up to speed. Is there anything else, Cindy, dear?"

"I'm off to interview Dorian and Jim Morley. This is a heads-up."

"Thanks," Conklin said.

"Off you go," I said to Cindy. "Have fun."

"You're not mad about anything?"

"Not at all. Thanks for the list." I waggled my fingers.

"See you later," she said to Conklin. I turned my face when she touched his cheek tenderly and kissed him. When Curlilocks had gone, I lifted my coffee, opened the file folder, and spread the morgue pictures of Elaine and Lily Marone out on the desk.

"Let's get back to work," I said to Conklin. "What do you say?"

I hung icicles from every word.

Chapter 56

"I TOLD HER nothing," Conklin said to me.

"Whatever," I said back. My mind was splitting, I think, literally. Hello Kitty. Lipstick Killer.

Lipstick Killer trumped everything.

"I didn't even mention the Morleys to Cindy."

"I believe you. It's over. She's going to run the story about Kitty being female, and the phone lines are going to burn up all over again."

"Cindy got a tip from one of the Morleys' friends. She did it all herself."

"Can we please move on?"

I didn't want to believe Conklin hadn't spilled the new info to Cindy, but I did. I do. He's honest. We've been partners for more than a year and, in that time, I've put my life in his hands more than once—and he's put his in mine. Crap. Images of the two of us working through bombings and firestorms and covering each other while trading shots with homicidal punks washed over me.

We had a bone-deep connection as partners, and then there was what Claire called the "other thing."

There was still a lot of spark in our relationship that had never been fully resolved. I remembered us grappling half naked on a hotel bed, an action that I'd stopped before it was too late. I recalled confessions of feelings. Promises to never discuss them again, that we had to keep our relationship professional, that it was the best and only way.

And now Rich was head over heels in amour with Cindy. That had to be why I was being a bitch. Had to be that, because I love Joe. I love him a lot—and Cindy and Rich are perfect together.

I took apart my stack of doughnuts and gave the chocolate one to Conklin.

"Wow. The chocolate one. For me?"

"I'm sorry. I'm hormonal. All the time."

"Just take it easy on yourself, okay, Linds?"

"I'm trying."

Conklin got up from his seat, came over to my side of our abutting desks, and sat in the chair Cindy had just vacated.

"Are you sure about Joe?" he asked me.

I was mesmerized for half a second. Conklin's good looks have that effect on me, and there's also something about the way he smells. Whatever the heck soap he uses.

"I'm sure," I said, looking away.

"He's the one?"

I nodded and said, "He's the one."

I felt Conklin's lips on my cheek, right there in the squad room, a decidedly unpartnerlike gesture, but I didn't care if anyone saw it.

"Okay, then," he said.

He went back to his chair and put his feet on the desk.

"If Hello Kitty's a female, what changes? Why would she shoot Casey Dowling?"

Chapter 57

IT WAS THEIR lunch break, and Sarah had left the building first. Now Heidi entered the diner and saw Sarah at a booth near the window.

Heidi broke into a smile, waved, and slid across the red leatherette banquette so she could sit next to Sarah and hold her hand. She kissed Sarah quickly, then looked over her shoulder, making sure there were no other teachers around.

"Happy birthday, darling," Sarah said. "You're a flirty thirty."

Heidi laughed. "I don't feel any different than when I was twenty-nine. I thought I would."

Menus were brought to the table and hot open-faced turkey sandwiches were eaten quickly because the lunch break was short and there was a lot on their minds. Heidi blurted, "If we could be together for real, without being afraid of getting fired, or of Terror or Beastly going ballistic, do you think we'd feel differently about each other?"

"You mean, would we care less about each other if we felt safe?"

"Yeah."

"No. I think it would be better. Will be better. That's a promise. Look, Heidi—"

Three waitresses came out of the kitchen, the one in front holding the cake, cupping her hand in front of the thirty small pink candles. The waitresses clustered at the head of the table and sang, "Happy birthday, dear Heidi. Happy birthday to you."

Applause sounded up and down the length of the narrow diner, and Heidi looked at Sarah, squeezed her hand, and then blew out the candles, every one of them on the first try.

"Don't tell me what you wished for," Sarah said.

"I don't have to. You know."

The two hugged, Sarah's heartbeats picking up

speed as she thought about the gift in the pocket of her jeans.

"I have something for my birthday girl," Sarah said. She dug into her pocket and came out with a packet so small only something really good could be inside. Heidi exchanged a mischievous glance with Sarah, peeled away the silver wrapping paper, and held the small leather box shaped like a round-topped trunk.

"I can't guess what this is," she said.

"Don't guess."

Holding the box in both hands, Heidi pried up the lid, then took out the chain and the pendant, a brilliant yellow, very faceted stone. Heidi gasped and flung her arms around Sarah's neck, asking her to please help her put it on.

Sarah beamed, moved Heidi's soft red hair off the nape of her neck, and connected the clasp. The bead guy at Fisherman's Wharf had done a wonderful job of fitting the stone into the new setting, not asking questions or even looking at her as he took the twenty dollars for the work.

"I love this. It's the most beautiful gift, Sarah. What kind of stone is it?"

"It's a citrine, but I think of it as a promise stone."

Heidi looked into Sarah's eyes and nodded.

Sarah touched the gem hanging sweetly from Heidi's neck and told herself that she would do the last job on her list, that she would hook up with a fence, that she would get Heidi and Sherry and Steven out of San Francisco, that somehow she and Heidi and the kids would stop being afraid every single day of their lives.

Chapter 58

THE REPLY TO the Lipstick Killer's "ransom letter" ran in the *Chronicle,* and within hours, the planet slammed on the brakes and all eyes became fixed on San Francisco. Media of every type and stripe materialized in satellite vans and on foot, surrounding the Hall of Justice and the Chronicle Building, swamping Tyler's phone lines with requests for interviews and dogging cops and newspaper employees on the street. Every man, woman, and child with an opinion and a computer fired off letters to the editor.

Interviews were denied, and the mayor pleaded with the press to "let us do what we need to do. We'll provide full disclosure after the fact."

*

Rich Conklin, Cappy McNeil, and I were embedded at the *Chronicle,* charged with screening out the garbage from the real thing: a reply from the killer with instructions on how to deliver two million in blood money in exchange for leaving San Francisco alone.

It was a sickening lose-lose situation that could only turn in our favor if we trapped the murderer. We had a simple plan. Follow the money.

At 2:15 in the afternoon, the mail cart arrived on the executive floor, carrying a fat brown envelope addressed to H. Tyler. I put on latex gloves and said to the mailroom kid, "Who delivered this?"

"Hal, from Speedy Transit. I know him."

"You signed for it?"

"About eight or ten minutes ago. I rushed it right up."

"What's your name?"

"Dave. Hopkins."

I told Dave Hopkins to go down the hall and ask Inspector McNeil, the big man in the brown jacket, to interview Hal pronto. Then I called out to Conklin, who exited the cube across the hall

227

and followed me to Tyler's doorway.

I said, "Henry, this could be it. Or it could be a letter bomb."

Tyler asked, "Do you want to drop it in a toilet or open it?"

I looked at Conklin.

"I feel lucky," he said.

I placed the packet in the center of Tyler's leather-topped desk. We all stared at the envelope with Tyler's name and the word "URGENT" in big black letters. Where the return address should be were three letters written in red: "WCF."

We'd withheld the killer's specific signature from the press, so there was little doubt in my mind that this packet was from him. Tyler picked up a letter opener, slit the envelope, and tilted it gingerly until the enclosed objects slid onto his desk.

Item one was a phone. It was a prepaid model, the size of a bar of hand soap, complete with neck straps, a headset with earbuds, a chin mic, and a built-in camera.

Item two was a standard envelope, white, addressed to "H. Tyler." I opened it and shook out the folded sheet of white paper inside. The message was typed and printed out with an inkjet. The note read: "Tyler. Use this phone to call me."

There was a number and the signature: "WCF."

Chapter 59

"CAN YOU TRACE a call on a prepaid phone?" Tyler asked.

I shook my head. "Not effectively. There's no GPS device, so there's no way to track the phone's location, either."

Tyler picked up the cell and dialed the number. I stooped beside him and put my ear next to his. There was ringing, and a man's voice said, "Tyler?"

"Yes, this is Henry Tyler. To whom am I speaking?"

"Do you have what I asked for?"

"I do," said Tyler.

"Turn on the phone cam. Show me the money."

Henry lifted a briefcase to his desk, opened the hasps, and pointed the phone at two million dollars in neat bundles. He snapped off a shot, then asked, "Did you receive the picture?"

"Yes. I asked you to choose a go-between."

"I'll be your contact," Tyler said.

"You're too recognizable," said the killer.

"I have a good man in ad sales," Tyler said, looking at Conklin. "And against my wishes, my secretary has volunteered."

"What's her name?"

"Judy. Judy Price."

"Put Judy on the phone."

Tyler handed the phone to me. I said, "This is Judy Price."

"Judy. This phone can stream video to my computer for three hours. I hope we can conclude our business in less time than that. Use the neck straps and wear the phone with the camera lens facing out. Keep it on until I have the money. I'll direct you as we go. Do you read me?"

"You want me to keep the phone on and wear it facing out so that it sends streaming video to you."

"Good girl. Hesitate to follow my directions,

screw with me in any way, and I'll hang up. After that, I'll kill a few more people, and their deaths will be on you."

"Hey, what if I lose service?" I asked.

"I'll call you back. Make sure the line is available. Don't try any stupid phone tricks, Judy."

"What should I call you?"

"Call me 'sir.' Are we clear?"

"Yes, sir."

"Good. Now hang the phone around your neck and do a little pirouette so I can see who's with you."

I turned on my heel, panning the office.

"I recognize Tyler. Who's the other guy?"

"That's Rich in ad sales."

"Turn on the speakerphone," the killer said.

I located the speaker button and turned it on.

"Rich, do not follow Judy. That goes for you, too, Tyler. And it goes without saying, if I see cops, anything that makes me think that Judy is being followed, I'll hang up. Game over. Understand?"

"Yes."

"Point the camera at yourself, Judy."

There was a pause. Longer than I expected. Then the killer's voice was back.

"Nice rack, Judy. And let's hope you're a smart blonde. Now connect the headset to the phone and put in the earbuds. Can you hear me?"

"Yes."

"Okay, sweet stuff, take the elevator down to the street. When you get to the corner of Mission and Fifth, I'll give you instructions."

"I can hardly wait," I muttered.

"You're coming in loud and clear," the killer said with an edge in his voice. "I'm warning you again, Judy. This is a lucky break for the city. Don't screw it up."

Chapter 60

THE PHONE HANGING from my neck felt like an explosive charge. The Lipstick Killer could see everything I saw, hear what I was hearing and saying, and if that vile, crude psychopath became unhappy, he'd cut down more innocent lives.

We'd been warned.

I walked out of the Chronicle Building into a dull gray afternoon. I took in the shoppers and the yellow-light runners, and wondered if the Lipstick Killer recognized the unmarked cars on Fifth and Mission. I saw Jacobi and Brady, Lemke and Samuels and Chi.

By now, Conklin had put out the word that I was the go-between and working undercover. Still, to prevent a shout-out, I caught Jacobi's eye and, being careful to keep my hand away from the lens, pointed two fingers to my eyes and then to the phone, signaling to Jacobi that I was being watched.

That's when I glimpsed Cindy. Her eyes were huge, and she was hanging back against the wall of the Chronicle Building, looking at me as though I were heading for the guillotine. I was suffused with love for her. I wanted to hug her, but I winked instead, holding up crossed fingers.

She squeezed out a smile.

I turned back to the street and hefted Tyler's ZERO Halliburton case in my right hand. I was afraid, of course. Once I handed "sir" the briefcase, he wouldn't want a witness. Odds were good that he'd shoot me. If I didn't shoot him first.

I said into the microphone, "I'm on the corner of Fifth and Mission. What now?"

"Drop your handbag into the trash can. And show me."

"My handbag?"

"Do it, princess."

Because I was in my role as Tyler's secretary, I'd secreted my gun and my cell phone inside my shoulder bag. I dropped it into the trash can, then tilted the camera so the killer could see that I'd done it. That son of a bitch.

"Good girl," the Lipstick Killer said. "Now let's head out to the BART on Powell."

The Powell Street BART was a block and a half away. As I crossed Market, I saw Conklin coming up behind me outside of camera range and felt a rush of relief. I had no gun, but my partner was with me.

I made my way down the stairs and reached the platform for trains going out to the airport. BART trains are sleek bullets that sound a warning whistle when they come into the station—which was happening now.

Brakes screeched. Doors opened. I got into the train marked SFO and saw Conklin get into the same car at the far end. The train started up, and the killer's voice piped into my ears, breaking up slightly. "Pan the car," he said.

I swung my shoulders slowly, giving Conklin enough time to turn away. The train was slowing for the next stop when a canned voice came over the PA system. It announced the station—Civic Center.

The killer said, "Judy. Get out now."

"You said the airport."

"Get out now."

Conklin was wedged into a corner, dozens of people between the two of us. I knew he didn't see me leave until I was off the train and the doors were closing. I saw the worried look on my partner's face as the train pulled out of the station.

"Take off your jacket and put it in the trash can," the killer said.

"My house keys are in the pocket."

"Throw your jacket into the trash. Don't question me, sweetmeat. Just do what I say. Now, go to the stairs. On the first landing, pan around so I can see if anyone is following you."

I did it, and the killer was satisfied.

"Let's go, princess. We've got a date at the Whitcomb."

Chapter 61

I CAME OUT of the underground into Civic Center Plaza, a clipped, tree-lined park flanked by gilded government buildings, banks, and cultural institutions—a fine public place encroached upon by the hopelessly addicted.

I searched parked cars with my eyes, hoping to see backup as I walked from the BART station to the Hotel Whitcomb. I heard a car take a fast left onto Market and saw a plain gray Ford pull up on its brakes. I couldn't turn without showing the camera who was driving, so all I could do was hope that Jacobi or someone was on my tail.

I crossed Market to the Whitcomb, an elegant four-hundred-room Victorian hotel, and entered the opulent lobby, glittering with crystal chandeliers, marble floors underfoot, wood paneling everywhere, and humongous floral bouquets scenting the cool air.

My personal tour guide sent me with instructions to the Market Street Grill, a beautiful restaurant that was nearly empty. The trim young woman behind the restaurant's reception desk wore her dark hair pulled back and a name tag on her blue suit jacket reading SHARRON.

Sharron asked if I'd be dining alone, and I said, "Actually, I'm here to pick up a letter for my boss. Mr. Tyler. He thinks he left it here at breakfast."

"Oh yes," Sharron said. "I saw that envelope. I put it away. Hang on a minute."

The hostess dug inside the stand and, with a little cry of "I've got it," handed me a white envelope with "H. Tyler" written in marker pen.

I wanted to ask if she'd seen the man who'd left the envelope, but the killer's warning was loud in my head. "Screw with me in any way, and I'll hang up. After that, I'll kill a few more people, and their deaths will be on you."

I thanked the hostess and walked down the hallway from the restaurant toward the lobby.

"Open the envelope, sweetheart," the killer said, and, gritting my teeth, I did it.

Inside, I found a ticket stub and twenty-five dollars in crisp bills. The stub was marked TRINITY PLAZA. I knew the place, an all-day lot nearby.

"Having fun?" I asked the Lipstick Killer.

"Loads," he told me. "If you're bored, tell me about yourself. I'm all ears."

"I'd rather talk about you. Why did you shoot those people?" I asked.

"I'd tell you," he said, "but you know how the saying goes: then I'd have to kill you — Lindsay."

"Who is Lindsay?" I asked, but I was rocked. My stride faltered and I nearly stumbled down the hotel steps. How did he know my name?

"Did you think I didn't recognize you? Gee, princess, you're almost a celebrity around this town. I knew, of course, that they'd put a cop on this gig. But, to my delight, it's you. Sergeant Lindsay Boxer, my girl on a leash."

"Well, as long as you're happy."

"Happy? I'm ecstatic. So listen up, Lindsay. I'm just a Google click away from knowing where you live, who your friends are, who you love. So

I guess you've got an even better reason to make this a payday for me, don't you, sweetmeat?"

I pictured Cindy in the camera's eye, Conklin, Joe working in his home office, Martha at his feet. I saw myself with my Glock in my hand, sights lined up between the no-color eyes of a guy in a baseball jacket. I squeezed the trigger.

Problem was, I didn't have the Glock.

Chapter 62

"YOU'RE QUIET, PRINCESS," said the voice in my ear.

"What do you want me to say?"

"No, you're right. Don't think too much. Just execute the mission."

But I was thinking anyway. If I saw his face and lived, I would quit the force if I had to in order to get the job done. I would look at all the thousands of photos of every former soldier, sailor, coastguardsman, and marine in San Francisco.

And if he wasn't living in San Francisco, I'd keep looking at photos until I found him, if it was the last thing I ever did.

But, of course, he wouldn't let me see his face and walk away. Not this guy.

I walked along Market, turned, and finally saw the parking lot. The guy in the booth was leaning against the back wall with his eyes closed, deep into his iPod. I rapped on the window and handed him the ticket stub, and he barely looked at me.

"That's twenty-five bucks," he said.

I pushed the bills at him, and he handed me the keys.

"Which car is it?" I said to the presence hanging from my neck.

"Green Chevy Impala, four cars down and to your right. It's stolen, Lindsay, so don't worry about tracing it to me."

The car looked so old, it could've been from the '80s, not the kind of junker someone would be in a hurry to report stolen. I opened the door and saw the brand-new Pelican gun case — long enough to hold an assault rifle — resting on the backseat.

"What's that for?" I asked the Lipstick Killer.

"Open it," he said.

Pelican is known for its protective cases. They are lined with foam, have unbreakable locks, and can withstand anything fire or water or an explosive blast can throw at them.

I opened the padded case. It was empty.

"Put the money inside," said the Lipstick Killer.

Again, I followed his directions, transferring the money from Tyler's special briefcase, stacking the bills, closing the locks, all the while raging—I was helping a psycho get away with holding up a city. I couldn't help thinking about the Nazis putting the screws to Paris in World War II.

"Slide Mr. Tyler's briefcase under the Lexus to your left," the killer said. "Just another precaution, princess. In case there's a tracking device in there."

"There's no tracking device," I said, but there was. Tyler's case had a GPS built into the handle.

"And take off your shoes," the killer said. "Slide them under the car with the case."

I did what he said, thinking how Jacobi would follow the GPS signal to this parking lot and find the case—and it would be a dead end.

"Feel like going for a ride?" my constant companion asked me.

"I'd love to," I said with false brightness.

"I'd love to, what?" said WCF.

"I'd love to, sir," I answered.

I got into the driver's seat and started the car.

"Where to?" I asked, sounding to myself as though I were already dead.

Chapter 63

"WELCOME TO THE mystery tour," the killer told me.

"Which way do you want me to go?"

"Take a left, princess."

I looked at my watch. I'd been wearing the devil around my neck for what seemed like forever, and I still knew nothing about him, nothing about what he intended to do. Since our genius "follow the money" plan had been canceled by the killer, my brain was on overdrive, trying to come up with another. But how could I? I didn't know where this guy was going to execute the drop.

I left the parking lot and drove past the Asian Art Museum. The killer told me to follow Larkin.

I glanced at the rearview mirror, seeing nothing that looked like an unmarked car.

No one was following me.

I took Larkin into the Tenderloin, threading the Impala through the roughest section in San Francisco, the dark streets crammed with hole-in-the-wall bars and girlie shows and rent-by-the-hour hotels. Jacobi and I had been shot in an alley not far from here, and we both almost died.

I passed streets I'd worked as a uniformed cop, a first-class pizzeria that I'd introduced Joe to a while ago, and a bar where Conklin and I sometimes came to wind down after a double shift. I turned onto Geary and drove past Mel's Drive-in, where I used to hang out with Claire when we were both rookies, the two of us laughing away our frustration at being females in a man's world.

I felt tears gathering in my eyes, not from the hoops the killer was making me jump through but from nostalgia, the aching memories of times with my good and beloved friends, and from the feeling that I was visiting sweet scenes from my past for the last time.

The disembodied voice of a man who'd wasted three young mothers and their small children spoke once again.

"Hang the phone over the rearview mirror, lens pointing at you."

I was at a stoplight at the intersection of Van Ness and Geary. As soon as I hung the phone on the mirror and looked into the pea-sized camera's eye, the Lipstick Killer said, "Take off your blouse, sweetmeat."

"What's this, now?"

"I told you. No questions."

I understood. He was checking me for a wire. First my purse, then my jacket, my shoes, and the briefcase. Now this.

I took off my blouse.

"Throw it out the window."

I complied. Not one of the skeezy pedestrians looked up.

"Do the same with your skirt."

"The light is green."

"Pull over and park. That's a smart girl," the killer said. "Take off that skirt and toss it. And now your bra."

I felt sick, but I had no options. I unhooked my

bra and dropped it out the window as directed. The killer whistled, a wolf call of appreciation, that sicko, and every part of my psyche hurt from the degradation. Not the least of which was that this murdering, child-killing woman hater had boxed me in and outmaneuvered the entire SFPD.

No one knew where I was.

"Good girl, Lindsay. Very, very good. Now, hang the phone around your neck and let's get going. The best is yet to come."

Chapter 64

I URGED THE old Impala up and down winding roads, then onto Lombard, the most curvaceous road of all, a tourist magnet that rose upward, cresting at Hyde, giving me a billion-dollar view, the reason why San Francisco should be one of the seven wonders of the world.

I've seen this panorama again and again, but this was the first time I'd failed to be dazzled by the full expansive sight of San Francisco Bay, Alcatraz, Angel Island—and then, in a flash, I was hurtling down the steep, twisting plunge of Lombard Street.

There were more directions in my ear, commentary about how cool it felt to let me do the driving while he got to sightsee and think about his money. Meanwhile I was stopping at every cross street, hunching my shoulders, praying that no one would notice a bare-breasted woman heading down one of the most scenic drives in the nation.

I checked my mirrors and swiveled my head at intersections, looking for Jacobi, Conklin, Chi, anyone.

I'll admit it. For an irrational blazing moment, I got mad. It's one thing to put your life on the line for a cause you believe in. It's another thing to be used as a robot for a killer, to be the lone sacrifice in an action you don't believe in — in fact, one you think is insane.

The killer spoke again. He told me to double back toward the Presidio, and I did it, continuing on Richardson, taking the ramp leading to the Golden Gate Bridge.

Were we leaving town?

My anger dissipated as I came back to myself, realizing that the squad was frantic to know where I was. How could they find me when I was driving an old green Impala?

The Lipstick Killer had stopped joking and was all business as I joined the high-speed river of traffic heading across the bridge. The needle on the gas gauge was hovering over the E.

"We need to fill up the tank," I said.

"No," the killer told me. "We'll be at the center of the bridge in about a minute. I'll tell you when to pull over."

"Pull over? There's no stopping on the bridge."

"There is if I tell you to," he said.

Chapter 65

SWEAT POURED INTO my eyes as the killer counted down from ten to one.

"Pull over now," he said.

My turn signal had been on since I got onto the Golden Gate Bridge, but anyone who saw it would have thought I'd left it on by accident.

"Pull over!" he repeated.

There was no actual place to stop, so I slowed, then braked in the lane closest to the handrail that acted as a safety line between the road and the narrow walkway.

I put on the hazard lights, listening to their dull clicking and imagining a horrible rear-end crash that could kill the occupants of the oncoming car and crush me against the steering wheel. I reduced my odds of making it from fifty-fifty to ninety-ten against. How could it be that today was my day to die?

"Get the case from the backseat, Lindsay," the killer told me.

I undid my seat belt, reached behind me for the long, awkward case, and hauled it into the front seat.

"Good. Now get out of the car."

It was pure suicide to exit on the driver's side. Cars whizzed past me at high speeds, some honking, some with drivers screaming through their windows as they passed. I angled the gun case, reached the passenger-side handle, pulled up on it, and kicked open the door.

I was almost naked, yeah, but I couldn't wait to get out of that car. I banged my shins with the case and negotiated the handrail, then my feet touched the walkway. Oncoming traffic was still swerving and honking. Someone yelled, "Jump. Jump," and there were more horns.

"Bridge security is tight," I told the killer. "There will be cops here any minute."

"Shut up," he said. "Go to the rail."

My head swam as I peered down into the

glinting water. He was going to make me jump. Approximately thirteen hundred people had leaped to their deaths off this bridge. Only twenty-odd jumpers had survived. It had come down to the wire, literally and figuratively. I was going to die, and I would never even know if I'd saved anyone — or if the killer would take the money and keep on killing.

And how was he going to get the money anyway?

I stared down at Fort Point, just under the south end of the bridge, and my gaze drifted along the Crissy Field shoreline. Where was the killer? Where was he? And then I saw a small motorboat coming out from Fort Baker, at the foot of the north tower, on the far side of the bay.

"Time to say good-bye, Lindsay," said the voice in my ear. "Drop the phone over the side and then send the case over. Keep up the good work, princess. Everything will be fine if you don't screw it up now."

The wind blew my hair across my face as I dropped the phone, then cast the gun case over the railing. I watched it fall 260 feet straight down into the bay.

Chapter 66

THE GUN CASE hit the water, sent up plumes of spray, sank, then bobbed up again into view. As best as I could tell, there was one man in the motorboat piloting the small vessel through the chop toward the gun case.

I snapped out of my trance—I was free.

I stepped behind the rear of the Impala and put up my hand. The driver of a peacock-blue Honda sedan leaned on his horn as he flew past me, followed by a Corvette, the guy behind the wheel leering but not pulling over. What did he think? That I was a prostitute?

I held my ground out there on that highway in my panties, my hand in the stop position, every part of me prickling from the fear of being flattened by a driver with his head up his ass—and then a baby-blue BMW slowed, pulled ahead of the Impala, and braked.

I leaned into the passenger side. "I'm a cop. I need your phone now."

There was a gawking eighteen-year-old boy at the wheel. He handed me his phone, and I pointed to a newspaper on the seat beside him. He passed it to me, and I held the front section to my chest as I called Dispatch, giving my name and shield number.

"Lindsay! Oh God. Are you all right? What do you need? Where are you?"

I knew the dispatcher, May Hess, self-described Queen of the Bat Phone. "I'm on the bridge—"

"With that naked suicide?"

I barked a laugh, then caught myself before I went into hysterics. I told May to get a chopper over the bay PDQ and why—that I needed the coast guard to pick up a boater. May said, "Gotcha, Sergeant. Bridge Patrol will be at your location in thirty seconds, tops."

I heard the sirens. With the newspaper fluttering against my chest, I leaned over the railing and watched as the small Boston Whaler motored closer to the floating gun case. A chopper whirred overhead, and the pilot bore down on the motorboat, herding it toward the southern shore.

The Boston Whaler dodged left and right like a quarter horse at a roping competition, ducked under the bridge, and powered beneath it, the chopper following the boat under the bridge deck, crowding the vessel until it stalled off Crissy Field.

The Lipstick Killer bailed out of the boat and ran in slow motion through hip-deep water. And then a coast guard vessel closed in on him.

A bullhorn blared, telling the killer to hit the ground and keep his hands in full sight. Squad cars tore down the beach and surrounded him.

Game over, psycho.

Chapter 67

I WATCHED HARBOR Patrol pull the Pelican case out of the water, and then there was the deafening sound of sirens all around me.

I turned and saw a fleet of cars—unmarked and black-and-whites—screeching to a halt behind the Impala, and driving those cars were just about every cop I'd ever met, now piling out and heading toward me.

My attention was drawn to a Land Rover stopping in the opposite lane, somehow making it through the perimeter before the bridge was closed off. A bearded man jumped out of the driver's seat holding a camera with a long SLR lens. He started snapping pictures of me wearing a look of horror on my face, the

Chronicle plastered to my chest, pink panties and all.

To my left, a yell: "HEY!"

A man burst from the back of a police cruiser, a big hunka guy, built like a football player. He crossed the roadway to the man with the camera and shouted, "Give me that!"

The big hunka guy was Joe.

The camera guy refused to give it up, so Joe grabbed him by the throat, extracted the camera from his hand, and threw it over the rail. He left the dude on the hood of the Land Rover and shouted out over his shoulder, "Sue me."

Then the man I love ran toward me with a look of anguish on his face. He held out his arms, and I fell against him and began to cry. "We got him," I said.

"Did that bastard hurt you?"

"No. We got him, Joe."

"You sure did, honey. It's all over now."

Joe put his big jacket around me and folded me into his arms again. Conklin and Jacobi got out of a gray unmarked car and came over to where I stood with Joe, asking in unison, "Are you okay, Lindsay?"

"Never better," I chirped, my cheeks wet with tears.

"Go home," Jacobi said. "Clean up. Have a meal, then come back to the Hall. We'll take our time booking that freak. Should take us about three hours to print him and do the paperwork. He's all yours, Boxer. No one will talk to him before you do.

"Good job."

Chapter 68

MY HAIR WAS still wet from my shower when I arrived back at the Hall, geared up and ready to confront the guy who'd humiliated me, terrified me, and killed six innocent people.

I walked to Jacobi's office and said, "What have we got?"

"His ID says he's Roger Bosco, former Park Service employee, currently a maintenance man at the San Francisco Yacht Club. No military background, no sheet of any kind. He hasn't asked for counsel."

"Let's do it," I said.

The observation room behind the glass was packed with cops, brass, and folks from the DA's office. The cameras were rolling. We were good to go.

The suspect looked up from his seat at the table when Jacobi and I walked into the interrogation room, and I was surprised at his appearance and demeanor.

Roger Bosco seemed older and smaller than the man we'd seen on the parking-garage tapes, and he looked confused. He turned his watery blue eyes on me and said, "I was afraid of the helicopter. That's why I tried to get away."

"Let's start at the beginning, Roger. Okay if I call you Roger?"

"Sure."

"Why did you do it?"

"For the money."

"Your plan all along was to collect the ransom?"

"What do you mean, 'ransom'?"

I pulled out a chair and sat down next to Bosco, trying to look behind the "little guy" act for a cocky, murdering psycho. Jacobi walked slowly behind us, turned, and walked back the other way.

"I understand that two million is a lot of

money," I said, keeping my temper in check, showing that I could be trusted, that the hours-long mystery tour from hell was forgiven.

"Two million? I was offered five hundred. I only got the first two fifty."

I looked up at Jacobi but could read nothing in his flat gray eyes. I ignored a new and sinking feeling. Bosco had been in a boat heading straight toward the money. It was indisputable.

"Roger. You've got to help me help you. Explain to me how you planned the killings. I have to say, you are brilliant. It took an entire police force to bring you in, and I respect that. If you can take me through every step, show us that you're cooperating fully, I can work with the DA on your behalf."

Bosco's jaw dropped. He looked at me in believable disbelief, turned to look at Jacobi, then turned back to look at me.

"I don't know what you're talking about. Honest to God, I didn't kill anybody, never in my entire life. You've got the wrong guy."

Chapter 69

IT TOOK HOURS of interrogation—me and Jacobi and Conklin calling people at their homes, going over papers in dark offices—in order to check out Bosco's credentials and alibi.

Yes, Roger Bosco was employed by the Yacht Club. His time was fully accounted for. He'd punched the clock and was seen at work when the Bentons, Kinskis, and Marones were slaughtered.

I took Bosco out of a holding cell and put him back in the box, this time with coffee, a ham sandwich, and a package of Oreos.

And he told Jacobi and me his story from the top: how a man had approached him at the dock, saying that he was a movie producer shooting an action film and needed a real, live stunt guy to pluck a package out of the bay.

Bosco told us that he was excited.

He said he told the guy that he could get a day off work and could use the Boston Whaler and would love to be in a film. So the "producer" instructed Bosco to idle the boat around Fort Baker and watch for a case that would be thrown from the bridge sometime in the afternoon.

He gave Bosco $250 in advance with a promise of the other half on delivery of the gun case, and he said that he'd be waiting for Bosco outside Greens Restaurant at Fort Mason.

Did Bosco seriously believe that this setup was for real? Was he dirty, or was he dim?

"This producer gave you his name?" I asked.

"Of course. Tony-something, starts with a 'T.' He was a regular-looking guy," Bosco continued. "He was about six feet tall and fit. I didn't even notice what he was wearing. Hey. Wait a minute. Wait a minute. I have his card."

Bosco's soaking-wet wallet was retrieved from booking, and the card was extracted from the billfold section and shown to me.

It was of the instant, do-it-yourself variety,

prepunched and printed on an ink-jet. It wouldn't have passed the credulity test of most people in this town, but Roger Bosco was very pleased that he could back up his story. He was grinning as if he'd found oil in his backyard.

"Look," Bosco said, stabbing the runny red logo with a callused forefinger. "Anthony Tracchio. WCF Productions."

Jacobi and I took it outside the room.

"The chief will love this," Jacobi said wearily, bagging the card. "I'm going to call him and tell him the Lipstick Freak is still out there. And, oh yeah, we've got the money."

Chapter 70

THEY WERE IN Cindy's bedroom, the light from the street coming through the blinds, painting bold stripes across the blanket. Cindy snuggled up against Richie and threw her arm across his waist.

"Oh man," Rich said. "I never thought I'd say this, but this has never happened to me before. I'm sorry, Cin."

"Hey, it's nothing. Don't worry, please," Cindy said, shaking him gently, kissing his cheek. "Are you okay?"

"I don't think so. I'm barely past thirty."

"You know what I think? You're preoccupied. What's on your mind, Rich? Quick. First thing that comes to you."

"Lindsay."

"I'll give you a million bucks if you take that back," Cindy said. She rolled away from Rich and stared up at the ceiling. Was Rich in love with Lindsay? Or was being her partner the same as being in love but in a different form?

This, she knew: Rich and Lindsay were tight. And she wondered again if their relationship was a red flag telling her that the tracks were out and she should get off the train.

"Ahh, that came out wrong." Richie pulled her back to him. "I wasn't thinking of her like that. It's about the Lipstick Sicko making her strip down. That, and how he could've killed her at any time. I'm her partner, Cindy, and I completely failed her."

Cindy sighed and relaxed in Rich's arms, strumming his flat belly lightly with her fingertips.

"You did everything you could do. I know what you mean, though. Lindsay winked at me outside the Chronicle Building on the way to her rendezvous with that freak. She was trying to assure me that she was going to be okay when there was no way she could know that. I felt utterly helpless."

"Exactly."

"I wanted to do something, but there was nothing I could do. Nothing."

Rich kissed her palm. "I'm always knocked out by the bravery of women," he said. "Like you, Cin. Working 'crime.' Living here."

Cindy's mind flashed over the "living here" part. She'd moved to this sunny apartment in the Blakely Arms, a great building in a borderline neighborhood, only to learn after her furniture arrived that someone was killing residents of the building.

"I'm scared all the time," Cindy said. "What you're calling bravery, that's me pushing back against my fear of everything. That's how I take care of myself."

"Is that what you want? To take care of yourself?"

"Sure. But that doesn't mean I want to be alone."

"No, huh?"

Rich pulled her tight, and she tilted her head back so she could look into his gorgeous face. She cared about him so much, it almost hurt.

"We ought to bunk together, you know?" Rich

said. "I'd feel better if you weren't here at night by yourself."

"You want to move in so you can protect me?"

"Wait, wait. What I mean to say is, I'm crazy about you, Cindy. Dating and so forth, it's great. But I want to be with you. I want more."

"You do, huh?"

Rich grinned at her. "Scout's honor. I sure do."

Chapter 71

SARAH'S ARMS BURNED so much, the pain was like fire, only *worse*. But she maintained the static hang from her chin-up bar until her muscles simply refused to obey any longer.

She dropped to her feet and shook out her hands for five minutes. Then, workout over, she went into the living room and settled into Trevor's ugly but incredibly comfortable recliner. She opened her laptop and was grading tests, half listening to the TV, when she heard Kathryn Winstead, Crime TV's most appealing reporter, engaging Marcus Dowling in an emotional interview.

Looking at Dowling, Sarah felt a shock of pure hatred. Still, she dialed up the sound and studied how much the monster had changed. Dowling had grown a beard and lost weight, and although he looked haggard, he still had the formidable presence of a movie star as he played the grieving husband role to the max.

Dowling's voice cracked and he even stammered as he told Kathryn Winstead that he was "empty inside."

"I wake up soaked with sweat," Dowling told the reporter. "For a m-m-moment, I think I've had a nightmare and I turn to where Casey should be lying beside me, and then it all comes back and I remember her c-c-calling out to me, 'Marc! Someone is in the room.' And then the shots. *Bang. Bang.*"

Sarah grabbed the remote and rewound the DVR.

What did he say?

She listened again as Dowling quoted Casey calling out to him. As far as Sarah knew, he had never gone public with Casey's last words before. The funny thing was, Casey *had* screamed out for her husband. That was true.

But there had been no shots.

Sarah put her laptop aside and went to the

kitchen. She washed her face under the faucet, got a bottle of tea out of the fridge, and gulped it down. That movie star had balls the size of coconuts. He was counting on her not to come forward because no one would believe her if she did. It would be Marcus Dowling's word against hers—and she was a thief.

Sarah returned to the TV, wound back the interview, and watched a sympathetic Kathryn Winstead say to Dowling, "And the police still have no suspects?"

"I haven't heard from them in several days, and meanwhile Casey's killer is still out there with a fortune in jewels."

Sarah snapped off the TV.

This was classic Samson and Delilah.

"Terror" wouldn't be home for two hours, and if she used that time efficiently, she'd be able to give Marcus Dowling a haircut. She couldn't allow him to get away with murder.

Chapter 72

SARAH HEADED TOWARD the phone kiosk at Fisherman's Wharf, one of the largest tourist attractions in the state. Families and herds of students parted around her, surging toward the shops and restaurants at the Cannery, no one even glancing at the young woman in gangsta shorts and a pink "Life is good" sweatshirt pressing quarters into the pay phone.

She tapped the buttons. The tip-line operator answered and switched the call to the Southern District Police Station, and Sarah asked to be connected to a Homicide inspector.

"What should I say this is about?"

"Casey Dowling," Sarah said. "I know who shot her."

"One moment, please. Sergeant Boxer is getting off the phone."

Sarah thought that the pay-phone call could be traced, but she'd be brief, and from her vantage point, she could melt into the crowd before a cop got anywhere near her.

"This is Sergeant Boxer," a woman's voice said.

"I'm the one who robbed the Dowling house. I didn't shoot Casey Dowling, but I know who did."

"What's your name?"

"I can't tell you that," Sarah said.

"Now there's a shock."

"Hello? Are you talking to me?" She put another quarter into the slot.

"Tell me something I can believe," said the cop, "or I'm hanging up."

"Listen," Sarah said, "I'm telling you the truth. I'm the burglar. I was looting the safe in the closet when Marcus and Casey came into the bedroom. They had a fight. Then they had sex. I waited for about twenty minutes until Marcus Dowling was snoring, and then I was bailing out the window when I knocked over a table. No one knows about the table, right? Is that proof enough?

Because Marcus Dowling keeps saying that Hello Kitty killed Casey—and I didn't do it."

"Okay. Okay, I hear you," Sergeant Boxer said, "but I need more than your anonymous say-so. Come in and make a statement. Then I can help you out of this jam so we can get whoever killed Mrs. Dowling."

Sarah could almost see that cop signaling to someone to trace the call. She'd already been on the line too long.

"Are you kidding? Come in so you can arrest me?"

"You don't have to come in. I'll come to you. Name the place, and we can talk there."

"Marcus Dowling killed his wife. There. Now we've talked."

Sarah disconnected the line.

Chapter 73

CONKLIN AND I hung up our phones at the same time and stared at each other over the wall of flowers on my desk.

"That was Hello Kitty," Conklin said. "That was for real."

"Why didn't we do a GSR test on Dowling?" I asked him.

"Because, damn it, I didn't order it," said Conklin.

"I was there, too," I said, throwing my stale tuna on rye into the trash. "So was Jacobi. We all blew it."

"We had orders," Conklin said. "Handle the movie star with kid gloves, and Dowling was having a heart attack, remember?"

"So-called heart attack," I muttered.

"And, by the way, he took a shower. And now we know why. Wash off the gunshot residue."

I gathered my hair up to the roots, found a rubber band, and made a ponytail. The last time I'd felt this incompetent, I was a rookie.

Last night Tracchio put out a statement that the Lipstick Killer hadn't shown up at the drop and that the letter from the killer that ran in the *Chronicle* had been a hoax. Cindy had written an editorial that ran in this morning's paper. In a spare Hemingway style, she called the Lipstick Killer a coward, and she said I was a hero. Since then, a truckload of flowers had arrived and filled up the squad room.

I didn't feel heroic. I felt like I'd done my best and even that wasn't enough.

Down at Golden Gate Avenue, the FBI was now working on the Lipstick Killer case along with a liaison from our squad — our trouble-shooter and floater, Jackson Brady. He was perfect for the job, freshly rested, hot to prove himself to Tracchio. He couldn't have dreamed up a better showcase for his years in the Miami PD. And, no kidding, I hoped he and the FBI had some fresh ideas about how to catch that psycho —because I was 100 percent sure that if he wasn't stopped, the Lipstick Killer would murder again.

Meanwhile, Jacobi was pressuring me to close the Dowling case, and that was okay. For the sake of our sanity and self-esteem, Conklin and I had to do it. The call from Kitty was our first and only break since Casey Dowling had been shot two weeks before. We finally had something to work with.

I said to Conklin, "Dowling told us he had sex with his wife before dinner, right? Now Kitty says they did it while she was looting the safe. That would be *after* dinner. So if that caller was for real"—I fit the pieces together as I talked—"we know why Dowling's clothes were negative for gunpowder and blowback. Marcus Dowling was naked when he shot his wife."

"You thought Dowling did it from the beginning," Rich said miserably.

"Doesn't matter. I dropped the ball."

Chapter 74

I CROSSED THE floor to Jacobi's office and stood in the doorway. He looked up, gray-faced, gray-suited, black-tempered. I told him about Hello Kitty's call.

"We found her story believable," I said.

"Did you put a trace on the call?"

"Warren, that's going to get us nothing. I heard a coin dropping into the box. She was at a public phone."

"Just do it, okay?" Jacobi growled. "What's wrong with you, Boxer?"

"I dunno," I said, throwing up my hands. "Stupid, I guess."

I went back to my desk. Conklin was looking past me, rocking in his chair, and when I snapped my fingers and called his name, he said, "Okay, we know what to do. Bear down on Marcus Dowling. He won't be expecting it."

My phone rang, and Brenda said, "Line one, Sergeant. That woman again. Says she was disconnected."

I stared at the blinking red button, then stabbed it and said, "This is Sergeant Boxer."

"Sergeant, don't write me off as a crank. I'm being falsely accused of murder. Do you know what was stolen from the Dowlings?"

"I have a list."

"Good. Then check it out. I took two opera-length diamond chains, three sapphire-and-diamond bracelets, a large diamond brooch in the shape of a chrysanthemum, and some other stuff, including an ornate ring with a big yellow stone."

"The canary diamond." There was silence. Then...

"It's a *diamond?*"

"What am I supposed to do with this information, Kitty? I need your statement, or I've got nothing."

9th Judgement

"You're a Homicide inspector. Do your job and leave me out of it," she said, and she hung up again.

Chapter 75

YUKI WAS PULLING into the garage under her apartment building when her mobile rang. The caller ID read "Sue Emdin," the woman she and Casey Dowling had both known at Boalt Law. Emdin was the "tough beans" type, but when she spoke now, Yuki thought her voice was strained to cracking.

"Sue. What's wrong?"

"Plenty. I saw Marcus having dinner with a woman in Rigoletto's. It's a dark, six-table Italian place on Chestnut, home-style cooking and not Zagat rated. They were in the back corner, laughing and canoodling. It wasn't a consolation dinner. Not in my book anyway."

Yuki nosed the car into her spot, turned off

the engine, got out, and headed to the elevator. Sue was filling in her report with color commentary.

"I wish you could've seen this girl. Tight little skirt, V-neckline down to her navel, showing off her great big bouncy boobs."

"Dowling had a hot date, you're saying?"

"Hot and a half with whipped cream on top. My husband would kill me for doing this, Yuki. He would say it's none of my business, but after the funeral? After that eulogy Marcus gave? Well, it was a performance, and ever since I swore to you that he didn't do it, I've been worried that I was wrong about him. For God's sake, what if he did kill Casey and I vouched for him? Makes me sick just thinking about it."

"Okay, I understand. Still, Marcus having a date is poor form, but it's not criminal."

"I'm not so sure."

"What does that mean, Sue?" Yuki's voice went up an octave. "What do you mean, exactly?"

"I've been following Marc since the funeral. I follow him all the time. Yuki, I had to do it. I was hoping he was the man I said he was, but another part of me was saying that he did kill Casey and that I was so under his spell, I didn't see it. Casey told me she thought he was seeing someone, remember? Oh my God, I can't stand it. Tell me I'm crazy and put me out of my misery, or do something for poor Casey."

Yuki juggled her handbag and briefcase. What had she created by talking to Sue Emdin? Her hands were shaking as she got out her keys and opened her front door. "Where are you now?"

"Outside his house. I've been here for over an hour. Babe-a-licious is still with him, and if you ask me, she's not going home. Not tonight anyway."

"Tell me again. What does this prove?"

"It proves that all of Marc's talk about how heartsick he is over losing Casey is bullshit. If he's lying about that, it means he could be lying about everything."

"What kind of car are you driving?" Yuki asked.

"Gold Lexus. I'm parked right across the street from his house."

"Nobody would notice a car like that."

"His neighborhood is full of them."

Yuki put down her briefcase, kicked off her heels, and looked for a pair of flats. She was as crazy as Sue.

"I'll be there in twenty minutes," she said.

Chapter 76

MY THIRD CUP of coffee was still hot when Yuki walked through the gate in the squad room at nine thirty a.m. and made a beeline to where I sat behind my floral barricade.

"I might have something on Marcus Dowling," she said.

Conklin got up, gave her his chair, and said, "You have our complete attention."

Yuki told us in one long run-on sentence that Casey's school friend, Sue Emdin, had been tailing Dowling for more than a week and had seen him last night in a restaurant made for clandestine meetings, having dinner with a woman who was more friendly than friend.

"Sue followed them from the restaurant, then

called to tell me she was staking out Dowling's house. I went to sit with her."

"Jesus, Yuki."

"Just listen, okay? No laws were broken. At about eleven last night, Dowling and this woman came out of the house, falling all over each other. She's in her late twenties, early thirties, Pilates body, long cover-girl hair. Totally gorgeous."

"You're saying, totally his girlfriend," Conklin said.

"So it would seem. Dowling helps said blonde into his car and then off they go."

"And you're following them?" I said.

"Well, yeah."

"Really, Yuki," I said, flipping my ballpoint into the air. "That was nuts and dangerous and you know it. Everyone wants to be a cop, but it beats the hell out of me why."

"It's a glamour job, right?" Yuki cracked, waving a hand to indicate the splendor of our grimy, gray-on-gray bull pen.

"So you're outside his house. What happened after that?" I asked.

"Okay, so we followed Dowling's car to Cow Hollow," Yuki said. "The car stops, and we have to drive past it, of course. We take a spin around the block, and on the return lap, I see Totally Gorgeous walking by herself to this extremely nice house. Dowling stayed in his car. He didn't leave until his girlfriend went inside, but the point is, he didn't walk her to the door. Clearly he didn't want to be seen."

Yuki paused for breath, took out a business card, and flipped it over so I could see the address she'd written on the back.

Conklin said, "We have his phone log."

I typed the address Yuki gave me into the computer and came up with a name and a phone number.

"Graeme Henley," I said to Conklin, and read him the number.

My partner scrolled down his computer screen. "It's here. He called that number three or four times a day all last month."

"Graeme Henley is probably not a woman," I said.

"So the girlfriend is married," Yuki said. "That's why he stayed in the car. Lindsay, Casey thought Marc was seeing someone. If he was, if he was serious, if he couldn't get rid of Casey...the girlfriend could be a motive."

"There's something else," I told Yuki. "I've got a witness who says Casey Dowling was alive when Hello Kitty left the Dowling house."

"You've got a signed statement?"

"It's an anonymous source but credible."

"Huh," said Yuki. "You have an anonymous but credible source who says Casey was alive when Kitty left the Dowling house. Who could that be? Oh my *God*. Kitty called you?"

"Uh-huh, and she told me things only Kitty could know. Have we got probable cause for a wiretap warrant?"

"It's a stretch," Yuki told us. "I'll go to work on Parisi. I'm not promising, but I'll give it everything I've got."

Chapter 77

YUKI GOT IT done.

A signed warrant for a wiretap was in my hands by lunch the next day, and within hours there was a tap on a phone circuit a couple of blocks from Dowling's house. Effective three o'clock in the afternoon, Dowling's phone calls were being routed through a small, windowless room on the fourth floor of the Hall.

The room was empty but for two Salvation Army-quality desks and chairs, a bank of file cabinets, and an outdated telephone book.

Conklin and I brought coffee and settled in behind a locked door. I was keyed up and bordering on optimistic. The odds that Dowling would say something incriminating were a long shot—but a shot we actually had.

For the next five hours, my partner and I monitored Dowling's incoming and outgoing calls. He was a busy lad, having scripts overnighted from Hollywood, schmoozing with his agent, his lawyer, his banker, his manager, his PR person, his broker, and—finally—his girlfriend.

The conversation with Caroline Henley was laced with "darlings" and "sweethearts" from both ends of the line. They made a plan to have dinner together the next week, when Graeme Henley was on a business trip in New York.

Then, when I was sure the conversation was over, it got interesting.

"You don't know what this is like, Marc. Graeme knows something's wrong, and now he wants us to go into counseling."

"I understand completely, Caroline. You have to stall him. We've waited for two long years, darling. Another few months won't matter in the big picture."

"You've been saying that forever."

"Three or four more months, that's all," Dowling said. "Be patient. I told you it will work out, and it will. We need the public to get bored with the story, and then we'll be fine."

Conklin broke into a grin. "Two years. He's been seeing her for two years. It's not a smoking gun, but it's something."

Chapter 78

I CALLED JACOBI from Yuki's office and told him that Marcus Dowling had been having an ongoing relationship with a woman, not his wife, for two years.

"Go get 'em," Jacobi said.

Conklin and I drove to Caroline Henley's place, a modern two-story house only blocks from the Presidio.

Mrs. Henley came to the door wearing her blond hair in one long braid, black tights under a blue-striped man's shirt, a big diamond ring next to her wedding band. A couple of little boys were playing with trucks in the living room behind her.

I introduced myself and my partner and asked

Mrs. Henley if we could come in to talk, and she opened the door wide.

Conklin has consistently proved that he can get any woman to spill her guts, so once we were ensconced in overstuffed furniture, I turned the floor over to him.

"Marcus Dowling says you two are very good friends."

"He never said that. Come on. I've met him at a couple of cocktail parties is all."

"Mrs. Henley, we know about your relationship," my partner said. "We just need you to verify his whereabouts at certain times. We have no interest in making trouble for you. Or," he added reasonably, "we can come back when your husband is home."

"No, please don't do that," she said.

Caroline Henley told us to wait. She bent to talk to the boys, then took their small hands, walked them to a bedroom, and closed the door.

She came back to her seat and clasped her hands in her lap, then said to my partner, "Casey stifled him. She ground him down with her jealousy and her constant demands. Marc was waiting for the right time, and then he was going to divorce her and I was going to leave Graeme. We were going to get married. That's not bull, that's the truth."

I walked around the living room as Caroline Henley told Conklin "the truth." There were photos everywhere, standing on tables, framed on the walls. Caroline Henley was either at the center of every group shot or alone, wearing something small that showed off her figure and her beautiful face.

I wondered why she was attracted to an aging movie star twenty years' her senior. Maybe her vanity demanded more of a catch than a stock-broker *ordinaire*.

"So, if I've got this right, you and Marcus Dowling have been lovers for two years," Conklin said.

Caroline Henley looked stunned as she realized why we were there. "Wait a minute. Are you thinking he had something to do with Casey's death? That's crazy. I would have known. Marc's not capable of that. *Is he?*"

She clapped her hands to her mouth, then dropped them. She almost looked pleased when she asked Conklin, "You think he killed Casey for *me*?"

Back out in the car, I said to my partner, "So maybe he wanted out of the marriage but didn't have the guts to tell Casey. Then Kitty shows up in his bedroom, for Christ's sake. Dowling couldn't have planned it better."

"Another way to look at it," Conklin said. "Divorce is expensive. But, if you get away with it, murder is dead cheap."

Chapter 79

SARAH WELLS WAS dressed for her night job, black clothes and shoes, car pointed toward Pacific Heights. She hit the turn signal and took Divisadero as the light went red. A cacophony of horns blared, damn it. Brakes screeched, and she narrowly avoided a collision with a station wagon full of kids.

Oh my God. Focus, Sarah!

She should be thinking about the work ahead, but her mind kept drifting back to earlier that night, seeing the perfect blue fingerprints on the soft flesh of Heidi's arms, the still-vivid bite mark on her neck.

Heidi had tried to brush off the evidence of Beastly's attack. "He's out of control," she said. "But it's not his fault."

"Whose fault is it? Yours?"

"It's because of what he went through in Iraq."

"It doesn't make any difference what the reason is," Sarah had snapped. "You don't have to take it."

She hadn't meant to bark at Heidi, but she was angry and scared at what Pete Gordon could do. Heidi had to get away from Beastly for her own sake, and for the good of the children.

"I know, I know," Heidi had cried out, putting her head on Sarah's shoulder. "It can't go on."

No, it couldn't go on, and it wouldn't, Sarah told herself as she cruised along Bush Street. She was meeting with Lynnette Green, Maury's widow, next week. Lynnette had told Sarah that she'd buy the jewels and sell them herself. Sarah couldn't wait to cash out. Could not wait.

She turned on Steiner and again on California, then parked her Saturn at the Whole Foods parking lot, surrounded by other cars. She took a few minutes to make sure she had all her gear, then locked her wallet in the glove box, got out of the car, and locked that, too, now thinking about Diana King, her target tonight.

Mrs. King was a widowed philanthropist, a big

wheel on the charity circuit, frequently photo-graphed and written about in the glossies and every month in the *Chronicle*.

According to the Lifestyle page, Mrs. King was having a small engagement party for her son and future daughter-in-law that night in her home, a superbly restored cream-colored Victorian. And also superbly restored was Mrs. King's classic jewelry: Tiffany, Van Cleef, Harry Winston.

If Sarah could steal it, Lynnette Green would buy it and make it disappear. And then it would be over. Tonight's job would be Sarah's grand finale, her last haul.

A half dozen cars were parked in front of the King house when Sarah approached on her rubber-soled climbing shoes. She crept into the side yard, which was shielded from the neighbors by a tall privet hedge. She peeked through one of Mrs. King's ground-floor windows and saw guests at the dinner table, deeply involved in conversation.

Sarah's pulse sped up as she prepared herself for the climb, and then she caught a lucky break: an air conditioner on the first floor that was diagonally placed under the master bedroom.

Sarah told herself she would spend only four minutes inside the house. Whatever she grabbed would be enough.

Using the air conditioner as a foothold, she easily gained purchase, and then she was through the open bedroom window and inside the house.

Getting in had almost been too easy.

Chapter 80

SARAH STOOD JUST inside Diana King's rose-scented bedroom, checking for anything that could impede her speedy exit. She crossed the room and closed the paneled door leading to the hallway. Then she flipped on her light.

The room was about fifteen feet square, with deeply sloped ceilings and a dormer facing the street. Sarah panned her light over the antique furnishings and cabbage-rose wallpaper, then hit the dresser with her beam. She was ready to go through the drawers when she saw a dark figure with a light. "Jeez! Who?" she squealed, then realized that it was her own reflection in the mirror.

Sarah, get a grip.

She flicked her beam back around the room and picked up a dull gold gleam on top of the vanity. She moved closer and saw a mass of jewelry, just tons of it, lying on the warm cherrywood surface.

Sarah was already swimming in adrenaline, but the mound of gold topped up her tank. She opened her duffel and, using the side of her shaking hand, slid the jewelry into her bag. A few pieces, a ring and an earring, escaped and fell to the floor. Sarah snatched them up before they stopped rolling. She glanced at her watch.

She'd made a first-class score in just over three minutes. A record, her personal best—and now it was time to go.

Sarah crossed to the window and let herself down over the side of the house, once again using the air conditioner as a foothold. Feeling almost giddy, she threaded her way between the hedge and the house until she reached the dimly lit street.

She'd pulled it off.

She was outta there.

Sarah ripped off her headlamp and dropped it into her tool bag as she turned right on the sidewalk, heading for the next street — then she pulled up short. She'd patted herself on the back too fast. Sirens shrilled, and Sarah saw a cruiser take the corner and head straight for her.

How she'd been found out, or even if the police were coming for her, was irrelevant. Sarah was holding several hundred thousand dollars in jewels and a bagful of burglar's tools.

She couldn't get caught.

Taking off at a run, reversing her direction, Sarah cut through the backyard of the house to the west of Mrs. King's. Mentally marking the spot, she ditched the bag of jewels into a basement window well and kept running. She skirted what looked to be the makings of a backyard shed and dropped her tools into a bag of construction trash.

Still at a run, Sarah whipped off her hat and gloves and tossed them under a hedge. She heard the siren stop only yards away, and someone shouted, "Stop! This is the police."

Without her light, Sarah couldn't see where to run, so she dropped to her haunches and froze against the rough stucco wall of a house. Flashlight beams swept the yard, but the lights didn't touch her. Radios crackled and cops called out to one another, guessing at which way she had gone, and for those interminable minutes, Sarah hugged the stucco wall, fighting the urge to run.

When the voices faded, Sarah broke diagonally across a yard full of kiddie toys to a metal gate, which she opened. The gate latch clanked. A big dog barked behind a door. Security lights blazed.

Sarah skirted the reach of the lights, running through shadows into another yard, where she tripped over a garden cart, falling hard enough for her right shoe to fly off her foot. She felt for the shoe in the dark but couldn't find it.

A woman's shrill voice called out, "Artie, I think someone's out there!"

Sarah vaulted over a fence, then took off again, ripping off her black sweater as she ran. She pulled the hem of her neon-green T-shirt out of her pants as she came out of the shadows onto a street she didn't know.

Feeling nauseous and desperate, Sarah stripped off her other shoe and her socks and left them in a trash can at the edge of a driveway, then headed north at a steady pace in the general direction of her car.

That was when she realized, too late, that her keys were in her tool bag and she'd locked her wallet in the glove box.

She was shoeless and miles from home without a dime.

What now?

Chapter 81

THE BRIGHT WINDOWS at Whole Foods were in sight when Sarah heard a car slowly coming up behind her on the dark street. The vehicle crawled, keeping pace with her, its headlights elongating her silhouette on the pavement.

Was it the cops?

Half out of her mind with fear, Sarah fought her compulsion to turn toward the car. Panic would show on her face. And if it was the cops and they stopped to question her—she was cooked.

Who was it? Who was trailing her?

A horn blared and then tires squealed as the vehicle behind her peeled out and flew past, an old silver SUV with a jerk hollering out the window, "Sweet ass, baby!" Sarah lowered her head as whoops of laughter receded.

Her red Saturn was where she had left it. She could see, by peering through Whole Foods' front windows, that the store was nearly empty.

A sandy-haired boy was closing down the last open register. He looked up when Sarah approached. She said, "I locked myself out of my car. Could I borrow your phone?"

"There's a pay phone outside," he said, cocking a thumb over his shoulder. Then his expression changed.

"Ms. Wells. I'm Mark Ogrodnick. I was in your class about five years ago."

Sarah's heart revved up again and went into overdrive. Of all the stores in the world, how had she found the one place in Pacific Heights where someone knew her?

"Mark. Great to see you. May I borrow your phone? I have to call my husband."

Mark stared down at her bare feet, at the bleeding gash on her shin. He opened his mouth and closed it, then fished his phone out of his back pocket and handed it to Sarah. She thanked him and walked down the produce aisle, dialing and then listening to the phone ring several times. Finally Heidi picked up.

"It's me," Sarah said. "I'm at Whole Foods. I locked myself out of my car."

"Oh God, Sarah," Heidi said. "I can't come. The kids are sleeping."

"Where's Beastly?"

"He's out, but he could walk in at any minute. I'm sorry."

"It's okay. I love you. I'll see you soon."

"I love you, too."

Ogrodnick looked up and switched off the neon light in the storefront window. Sarah had no choice. She dialed her home phone number and, for the first time ever, prayed that Trevor would pick up.

"Sarah, where the hell are you?" Terror asked with a sharp edge in his voice.

Meekly, Sarah told him.

Chapter 82

AFTER TREVOR THREATENED her, drank, shoved her around, and collected his marital due, he finished a six-pack and went to bed. Red-eyed, sore, and frightened, Sarah sat in his chair, squeezing the exercise ball. She changed hands, working her fingers until they were nearly numb. Then she shook out her hands and booted up her laptop.

Once she was on the Web, she clicked on Google News and typed "Hello Kitty" into the search bar.

To Sarah's relief, there was no mention of the burglary at Diana King's house. Not yet. But Sarah was worried about the tools she'd ditched in her steeplechase through Pacific Heights.

Specifically, had she been wearing gloves when she changed the battery in her headlamp? She couldn't remember.

And so Sarah searched her mind for an out. She'd dumped the tools in a trash bag near that small construction site. Maybe if someone found it, he'd think, *Cool. Free stuff.* Or maybe the trash bag would be tied and simply taken out to the curb.

Sarah thought about all the other stuff she'd left behind like a trail of bread crumbs: her sweater and socks and shoes. By themselves, they were nothing. But if her prints were on the battery, everything else could be used to back up the charges against her.

Ladies and Gentlemen of the jury, if the shoe fits, you must nail her ass for twenty years without possibility of parole.

Sarah groaned and ran the cursor down the Hello Kitty page. She read a few articles about her burglaries and her growing infamy, taking no pleasure in any of it. A headache bloomed behind her right eye as she tapped into the canon of stories about the Dowlings. The most recent clips were all Marcus Dowling quotes and interviews, but as she scrolled to earlier pages, she found stories from the day after she'd done the Dowling job.

A headline grabbed her attention.

"The Sun of Ceylon Stolen in Fatal Armed Robbery."

Sarah flashed on a few words that had been almost forgotten since she'd spoken with Sergeant Boxer. The cop had said that the yellow stone was a diamond. Now it seemed the diamond had a name. After clicking on the link to the article, Sarah began to read.

"The Sun of Ceylon," a twenty-karat yellow diamond, was stolen from actor Marcus Dowling and his wife, Casey Dowling, who was killed in an armed robbery. When last seen, this showy stone was set in a handworked gold ring with 120 smaller white diamonds.

The Sun has a long history, marked with sudden death. Once the property of a young farmer who found it in a dirt street in Ceylon, the stone has passed from paupers to kings, leaving a trail of tragedy behind.

*

Sarah felt as if a fist had closed around her heart. She called up the history of the Sun of Ceylon and everything that had happened to the people who had owned it—a long list of financial ruin and disgrace, sudden insanity, suicide, homicide, and accidental death.

In her research on gems, Sarah had read of other stones like the Sun. The Koh-i-noor diamond, known as the "Mountain of Light," brought either great misfortune or an end to the kingdoms of all men who owned it. Marie Antoinette wore the Hope diamond, and she was beheaded—it was said that a string of death and misfortune followed the stone.

There were other gems that carried curses: the Black Orlov Diamond, the Delhi Purple Sapphire, the Black Prince's Ruby. And the Sun of Ceylon.

Casey Dowling had owned it. And now she was dead.

Sarah had given that stone to Heidi as a romantic gift—but what if it brought evil into Heidi's life?

Sarah had to ask herself, *Am I really this superstitious?*

Crossing your fingers and throwing salt over your shoulder were baloney. Still, call it stress, call it irrational—it didn't matter. Sarah felt it strongly. It was well-documented. People who owned cursed gemstones died.

She had to get that diamond back from Heidi before Pete really hurt her.

Chapter 83

THE POLICE CAR circled the parking lot at Crissy Field like a buzzard. Sarah stiffened as she watched the cruiser in her rearview mirror, seeing it loop slowly around the lot while she wondered if her former student Mark Ogrodnick had told the police that she'd been in Whole Foods, barefoot, scraped up, and looking scared.

Sarah held her breath and moved only her eyes, and then the black-and-white eased out of the exit and continued onto the boulevard.

God, Sarah, chill.

There's no way those cops could be looking for you here. No way!

Putting on her sunglasses, Sarah got out of the car. She crossed over the trail to the beach side of the walk and sat on an empty bench facing the water.

Weather was coming in, clouds obscuring the afternoon sun but not stopping the windsurfers, who were shouting to one another as they changed their clothes out there on the asphalt.

Zipping up her jacket, Sarah felt chilled inside and out. How do you tell someone you love that you've been leading a double life—and, in her case, a *criminal* double life? She had to get Heidi to understand that she knew stealing was wrong and dangerous, but if she could provide the means for all of them to escape Terror and Beastly, then she could live with what she'd done.

Sarah imagined Heidi looking at her as if she were an alien, gathering up the kids, getting back into her car, and driving off. Sarah crossed her arms over her chest and doubled over. It killed her to think of losing Heidi. If that happened, everything she'd done would be for nothing.

Sarah's cell phone rang. She answered it.

"Where are you, Sarah? We're in the parking lot."

Sarah stood up and waved. Sherry screamed,

"Sarah, Sarah," and ran to her mom's friend. Sarah lifted the little girl into her arms.

Heidi broke into a grin. She held on to her floppy hat and balanced Stevie on her hip, the wind blowing her skirt tight against her body. Heidi was so beautiful. And that was the least of why Sarah loved her.

Heidi came to her and hugged her with the kids in the middle, Sherry scrutinizing Sarah's face, asking her, "What's wrong, Sarah? Did someone hurt you?"

Sarah put Sherry down and started to cry.

Chapter 84

HEIDI AND SARAH crossed the picturesque bridge, over an inlet that ran from the bay into the pretty little nature park. Sherry took Stevie ahead toward the wooden dock and, grown-ups forgotten, gathered stones to throw into the water.

The two women sat together on a bench, and Heidi asked, "What's going on, sweetie?"

Sarah looked into Heidi's face and said, "There's no good way to tell you. I wanted to keep you out of it. I didn't want to involve you in any way."

"Wow," Heidi said. "You're really scaring me."

Sarah nodded and, looking down at her feet,

said, "You know about the cat burglar they call Hello Kitty?"

"That's the one who killed Marcus Dowling's wife, right?"

"Yeah, well, I didn't do it."

Heidi laughed. "Duh-uh. Of course not. What are you talking about?"

"Heidi, I'm Hello Kitty."

"Shut up! You are not!"

"Would I make this up? Heidi, believe me, I'm the cat burglar. Let me get this all out, and then I'll tell you anything you want to know."

"Okay. But — okay."

"I told you, my granddad was a jeweler," Sarah said. "But I didn't tell you he had a friend who was a fence. I heard a lot of stories when I was Sherry's age, just playing with stuff in my granddad's shop.

"So when I was thinking how to get us all out of here, I realized I could actually get rich quick. I started climbing the wall at the gym, getting strong, and I started researching potential targets, picking only people who could recover from the loss of their stuff. At first I wasn't sure I could do it.

"And then Trevor raped me."

Sarah swallowed hard, forcing her mind to skip past the memory.

"My first few burglaries were — easy," Sarah said. "I had a knack for it, and I could count on Terror to pass out in front of the TV long enough for me to do the job, come home, and get into bed before he woke up.

"Then there was the Dowling job."

Heidi looked stricken, as though she were trying to say something but couldn't find the right words. Instead she just stared. Sarah kept going. She told Heidi about Marcus Dowling's outrageous lies and about the next job — the one where Jim Morley came into the room when her hands were wrist-deep in his wife's jewelry. And then she went on to the robbery of Diana King, the last job she was ever going to do.

"It had to happen," Sarah said. "I thought I was home free. And then a cop car came out of the dark, shining lights on me, following me. So I ditched everything: the jewelry, most of my clothes, and — in a perfectly brilliant move — my tool bag with my car keys inside. When you couldn't come get me, I had to call Terror."

"I'm sorry, Sarah."

Sarah shook her head. "Not your fault. Anyway, Terror didn't like my answer to why I was locked out of my car and barefoot in Pac Heights," Sarah went on. "I couldn't think of a lie that wasn't frickin' totally laughable, and obviously I couldn't tell him the truth. So I said that I didn't answer to him. That I was entitled to have a life."

Heidi was murmuring, "Oh no, oh no."

"He accused me of sneaking out to be with a guy. And then he 'taught me a lesson.'"

Sarah pulled at the neck of her shirt and turned her head so that Heidi could see the fingerprints around her throat.

Heidi clapped her hand to her mouth.

"Oh my God, Sarah," she said. She put her arm around the woman she loved and drew her close. "Sometimes I wonder if I even know you."

Chapter 85

THE WARMING HUT is a bright-white snack and gift shack at the intersection of the Crissy Field and the Presidio, where the outstretched arm of the Golden Gate Bridge spans the bay.

Sarah and Heidi lunched on soup and sandwiches while the kids sat near the window, picking at their food and blowing bubbles into their drinks.

"There's something else," Sarah said. "That stone I gave you."

"Let me guess. It's hot."

"Very, very hot. It's a diamond. With a name and a freaky history."

Heidi pulled at her necklace so she could

look at it. "You said it was something else. A citrine."

"Its name is the Sun of Ceylon, and it comes with a curse."

"A curse? That's insane."

"I know, I know, but the stories go back three centuries. Hey, it belonged to Casey Dowling when her son-of-a-bitch husband killed her. What more do I need to say?"

Sherry came over and leaned against Heidi. "What's a curse, Mommy?"

"It's a wish for something — bad."

"Like if I wished something bad would happen to Daddy?"

"Sherry, Stevie is about to cry. Be a good girl and give him a hug."

"I don't want you to wear it anymore," Sarah said when Sherry had gone. "It's tempting fate, you know?"

"Really?" Heidi laughed. "This is tempting fate? My God, that's a riot." She unclasped the chain and handed the necklace to Sarah. "The Sun of Ceylon, huh? Well, it's a little flashy for me anyway."

Sarah said, "Thanks," took the pendant,

jammed it into her hip pocket, and forged ahead to the last of her story—her plan to meet with Lynnette Green and turn the jewels into cash for their plunge into a new life as a family of four.

"I have something to say, Sarah."

"Okay, but take it easy on me. I'm a wreck."

"I can hardly believe you did this."

"You're appalled. Go ahead and say it."

"I'm completely blown away. But I'm so grateful that you'd do this for us. You risked your life, Sarah. If the kids weren't here, I'd kiss you. I've never loved anyone so much."

"I love you, too."

"What now? You think the police are on to you?"

"It's possible," Sarah said, rubbing her temples. "That kid at the supermarket. He could tell the cops. A fingerprint could turn up on something I ditched. Time is running out on all fronts, Heidi. If we're going to jump outta here, we have to do it soon."

"I know. We're a team. Everything you do involves all of us now."

Sarah nodded and was quiet for a while as she

sorted through a number of options, every single one of them scarier than the last—but just as compelling.

"Sarah?"

"I know what to do."

Chapter 86

PETE GORDON HAD parked at the outer edge of the shopping center, beyond the lights and the security cameras, and was waiting now for Heidi and the kiddos to catch up with him.

Keyed up but in control, Pete was aware of everything around him: the smell of newly painted lines in the parking lot, the shoppers walking out to their cars, the lights at Mervyns and Toys "R" Us, and the deepening dusk of the sky.

The adrenaline charging through his veins sharpened his mind as he waited out the last minutes before he would execute the most critical phase of his plan. Once he'd eliminated the Three Stooges, he'd walk to his house and stretch out

327

in front of the TV. He'd be home before the cops were even called.

He ran the three little sentences of his letter to the *Chronicle* through his mind: "Believe me now? The price has gone up to five million. Don't screw up again."

He couldn't be any clearer than that.

The letter would run as the cops and the media were consoling him for his terrible loss, blaming yet three more "senseless murders" on the Lipstick Killer.

It was a brilliant plan, and he had to give himself credit, because he'd never get it from anyone else.

And with that, Pete heard Heidi yakking away and saw her in the rearview mirror bouncing the stink bomb on her hip as she pushed the shopping cart. He also heard another voice — damn it. It was that dog-faced Angie Weider, one of their neighbors, and here she was, pushing her brat in a stroller.

Heidi called out, "Bye," to Angie, then pulled up on the shopping cart, leaving it at the back of the car.

"Pete?"

Heidi opened the rear doors, strapped the kids in, and called over the seat back to him, "Petey, would you get the groceries?"

"No problem, princess. All you have to do is ask."

Pete pulled on his gloves, leaped out of the car, and opened the trunk lock, waiting as a vehicle sped out of the lot. When it was all clear, he stowed the groceries neatly beside the emergency road kit and the shoe box that held his loaded gun.

"Hey, Pete," Angie Weider called out to him, "you guys should come to dinner with us. We're going to the BlueJay Café."

"Another time, okay?" Pete said, dropping the gun back into the box, fury flooding through him, a tidal wave of hatred directed at that bitch who had destroyed both his opportunity and his alibi in one blow. He thought for a moment of killing her and her tot, but he could hear Heidi screaming and see Sherry running and he'd never be able to murder them all without being seen.

Heidi ignored him. "Kids, want to go out for dinner?"

Sherry sang her approval and the stink bomb

gurgled his. Pete slammed the trunk lid shut and, barely checking his temper, said, "You go ahead. There's a game on in ten minutes."

Heidi said, "Just remember to put the ice cream away, and I'll take care of the rest when I get home."

She grabbed the stink bomb out of his car seat, and Sherry skipped over to the Weiders' van. With a toot of the horn, they were gone.

Pete jerked the car into gear and backed out.

Change of plan. He wasn't going to go home after all.

Chapter 87

IT HAD BEEN a week since I'd stopped traffic on the Golden Gate Bridge with the front section of the *Chronicle* clasped to my chest, ten days since that psycho we call the Lipstick Killer had murdered Elaine Marone and her child. I could still feel the weight of the killer's cell phone hanging around my neck, could hear his jeers and gibes as he ordered me to disarm and disrobe myself on the way to the drop that never was.

I was relieved that the Feds had taken the Lipstick Psycho off our hands. The Dowling case was heating up. We had a wiretap transcript that could lead to probable cause. And in Evidence we had a climber's shoe, a Banana Republic sweater, and a bag of tools that probably belonged to Hello Kitty.

I liked the feeling of getting traction at last, so I was none too happy when Jackson Brady called at six that evening, saying the FBI had requested my help at a triple homicide.

Twenty minutes after Brady's call, Conklin and I were climbing the chilly ramp of a parking garage. It was several levels of a winding concrete helix that connected by an overpass to Pier 39, a gigantic mall full of restaurants and shops, the perfect place to disappear after bloody murders.

Brady introduced us to Special Agent Dick Benbow, a square-shouldered man of about forty with a crisp haircut and mirror-shined shoes. Benbow shook our hands, then walked us toward the scene, which was now being processed by a dozen Federal agents.

Benbow said, "Sergeant Boxer, no one knows this animal the way you do. I want to know what you see. What's the same? What's different? What's your theory of the case?"

My scalp tightened and every hair on my body stood up as we closed in on a young black woman lying under the glaring fluorescent lights, her eyes wide open and a bullet hole in the center of her forehead.

She was wearing expensive clothing: a long, printed designer skirt, a navy-blue jacket, a white blouse with tucks and fancy buttons. It looked like she was visiting here, not just going to the mall.

A tipped-over double-wide stroller lay six feet behind her. Two dead children were hidden by the stroller, but I could see a lot without taking a step: twin puddles of blood, a little foot wearing a small white shoe to the left of the stroller, the hand of another young child flung out to the right, a pacifier only inches away.

He might have reached for that small comfort before he died.

Benbow said, "The victims are Veronica Williams; her daughter, Tally; and her son, Van. They were visiting from LA. We've notified the family."

I held down a scream of outrage as I stood over the dead bodies of victims number seven, eight, and nine. It wasn't just murder. It was slaughter.

I stared helplessly at Benbow, then walked over to the Blazer with rental plates. The driver's-side door was hanging open, and lying on the ground was an expensive black leather handbag. It had disgorged a wallet, an open makeup bag, a pacifier, an airline-ticket folder, aspirin, a cell phone, and packets of moist towelettes.

I leaned into the vehicle. The light coming through the glass outlined the lipstick lettering and turned it black. Instead of three cryptic letters, there were six words, just as unfathomable.

WOMEN AND CHILDREN FIRST. GET IT?

No, I didn't get it. I didn't get it at all.

He was smart and slick, and he *hated* women and children, that much I got. But what set him off? How had he committed nine homicides without being noticed? How would we catch him?

Or would the Lipstick Killer case become one of those unsolved mysteries that haunt cops into their graves?

I said to Benbow, "No question, this is the same shooter. He's spelling out the acronym. It's his signature. I don't have a theory on this case. I wish I had one frickin' clue."

I put my back against a concrete pylon and called Claire, saying to her voice mail, "I'm at the

Pier Thirty-nine garage. Three more victims, two are little kids."

Claire picked up. She doesn't swear often, but she let loose an impressive stream of curses before saying she was on her way. As she hung up, I heard footsteps on concrete. I turned to see Jackson Brady coming up the ramp with two other men: a uniformed police officer and a wiry white male with graying hair. Brady's eyes had brightened, and there was a new expression on his face that gave me hope.

He smiled.

I felt storm clouds part and a godlike finger of light break through the concrete ceiling when Brady said to me, "This is Mr. Kennedy. Says he's a witness."

Chapter 88

SIX LAW ENFORCEMENT officers surrounded the man called Daniel Kennedy. We were standing so close we were pretty much sucking up his air, but he seemed glad for the attention. Kennedy said that he was a crime buff and had read everything about the Lipstick Killer. He told us that he was the owner of U-Tel, a telephone shop at Pier 39, and then he got into his story.

"A white guy in his early thirties came into my store," Kennedy said, "and right away, I thought he was wrong."

"Why was that?" Benbow asked him.

"He goes over to the rack of prepaid phones, picks one with a camera and a two-gig chip. Cheap prepaids fly off the shelves, but expensive phones? Who throws away an expensive phone? Anyway, this guy knows what he wants. And he keeps his head down, never even looks up when he pays."

"Was he wearing a cap?"

"Yeah, baseball cap, blue, no logo but a different jacket than the one in the artist's rendering on TV. This jacket was brown leather, kinda distressed, American flag on the right sleeve."

"Flight jacket," Conklin said. "What color was his hair?"

"Brown, what I could see of it. So after he buys the GoPhone, he leaves, and I tell my manager to take over for a couple of minutes."

"You followed the guy?" Brady asked.

"Sure did. I kept back a few yards so he wouldn't notice me, and pretty soon I see him talking to this pretty African-American woman with two kids in a double stroller. He was gesturing to her, like, asking if he could give her a hand with her packages.

"Then, damn it, my manager called asking me to sign off on a personal check for a big sale. I turned around for a minute, and when I turned back, I'd lost him—the place was packed, you know? I go back to the store, and next thing, there's sirens coming up the road. I turn on my police band and hear that there's been a shooting."

"Could you ID this guy from photos?" I asked.

"I can do better than that. Everything that guy did inside and in front of my store was recorded on high-quality digital media. I can make you a disk off my hard drive right now."

"Was he wearing gloves?"

"No," said Kennedy. "No, he wasn't."

"How'd he pay for the phone?" Conklin asked.

"Cash," Kennedy said. "I gave him change."

"Let's open your register," I said.

Chapter 89

MY CELL PHONE rang at some bleary predawn hour. I fumbled with it in the dark and took it into the living room so Joe could sleep. My caller was Jackson Brady. Despite the weariness in his voice, I caught his excitement as he told me he'd been at the crime lab all night watching the CSU dust every bill from U-Tel's cash drawer.

"You've got something?" I asked, daring to hope.

"Only some partial prints that match to a former marine."

"No *kidding*. That was your hunch."

"Captain Peter Gordon. Served in Iraq, two back-to-back tours."

I stood in my blue flannel pj's looking down on

the quiet beauty of Lake Street as Brady told me of this former marine officer who, after he was discharged, went off the radar. There was nothing unusual in his military record, no postduty hospitalizations—also no homecoming parades.

"After Gordon's discharge," Brady told me, "he returned to Wallkill, New York, where he lived with his wife and little girl for a couple of months. Then the family moved to San Francisco."

"So what do you think, Brady? You like him as our killer?"

"He sure looks like Lipstick," Brady said. "Of course the garage videos are crap, and what we've got from U-Tel isn't conclusive. Gordon bought a prepaid cell phone twenty minutes to an hour before Veronica Williams and her kids were killed—that's all. Can't do much with that."

"Wait a minute. Gordon was seen talking to Veronica Williams," I said. "She had two children in a stroller. Christ!"

"We don't know if the woman Kennedy saw was Veronica Williams. We've got six people screening all of the Pier Thirty-nine surveillance videos," Brady said. "Look, Lindsay, I'd love to pick him up, but when we do it, we want to nail him good."

Brady was right. I would've been giving him the same lecture if our positions were reversed.

"Anything on Gordon since he moved to San Francisco?"

"As a matter of fact, a neighbor called in a domestic disturbance twice, but no charges were filed."

"You have a picture of this guy?"

"It's old, but it's coming at you now."

The picture on my cell phone was of a man with bland good looks, about thirty, brown hair, brown eyes, symmetrical features, nothing remarkable. Was this the man who'd worn a two-tone baseball jacket and had hidden his face from the security cameras at the Stonestown Galleria? Wishing didn't make it so, but I felt it in my gut.

Pete Gordon was the Lipstick Killer.

I knew this was him.

Chapter 90

SARAH WELLS AND Heidi Meyer, along with a half dozen of their colleagues, huddled around the TV in the teachers' lounge during their lunch break. On the screen was a jumpy video of Chief Medical Examiner Dr. Claire Washburn attempting to drive away from the scene of the terrible shooting at the Pier 39 garage the night before.

The vehicle's egress was blocked by a crowd of onlookers made up of looky-loos, reporters, and the police, who had sealed off the entrance to the garage. A video camera focused on Kathryn Winstead of Crime TV as she shouted to Dr. Washburn, "How many people were shot? Was it another mother and child? Were the shootings done by the same killer?"

"Move aside. I'm not joking. Step back from the vehicle!" Dr. Washburn shouted back.

"Recently you told women to carry guns," Winstead continued. *The public needs to know.*"

"I meant what I said," Washburn answered, then blew a hole through the crowd with her horn and pulled out onto the street.

The scene switched back to the studio, Kathryn Winstead saying, "For those just joining us, we've obtained a security video from a Mr. Daniel Kennedy, the owner of U-Tel, a shop at Pier Thirty-nine. The man you see in this video appears to be the same one we've seen in the surveillance tape from the Stonestown Galleria garage. Sources close to the SFPD confirm that he may very well be the Lipstick Killer."

Heidi's mouth dropped open as she watched her husband buying a cell phone.

But there was a mistake. Pete wasn't the Lipstick Killer.

How could he be?

Sarah took Heidi's arm and walked her away from the TV, out of the lounge, and into the hallway. She asked, "Where was Pete last night?"

"Pete? We went shopping and then I went out

to the BlueJay Café with my neighbor...," Heidi said, her face blanched, her eyes wide with horror. "Pete said he was going home to watch the game. He was on the couch when I got there. He couldn't have done what they say."

"It's a short drive from your house to Pier Thirty-nine."

"We were at dinner for a while—*oh my God*. But it couldn't be him. I would know, wouldn't I?"

"Heidi, he's mean. He's abusive. He treats you and the kids... look, where does Pete go when he says he wants to be 'anywhere but here' and then disappears for hours? Do you know?"

"God. You're serious." Heidi looked into Sarah's resolute face, then her knees buckled. Sarah steadied her and said, "Heidi, Heidi, are you all right?"

"What if this is true? What am I going to do?"

"Where are the kids?"

"Sherry's in school. Stevie's at day care—unless, oh God. What time is it? *Pete picked Stevie up*. I've got to call the police. Where's my bag? I need my phone. I've got to call the police *now*."

Chapter 91

PETE GORDON WAS cleaning his gun in front of the TV, watching that video of him buying a phone at the mall.

The video had been all over the news for the last thirty minutes, and now a CNN talking head was saying, "sources close to the FBI have confirmed that this man is a person of interest in the recent killings in parking garages around our city. His name has not been released, and if you know or see him, do not confront him. He is classified as armed and very dangerous…"

"Why, thank you," Pete said, screwing his suppressor onto the barrel of his Beretta. He put the gun into his waistband and went out to the garage. His go-bag was already in the trunk, along with the emergency kits and a case of bottled water.

He got into the car, buzzed up the garage door, and immediately heard the sound of props twirling overhead. He couldn't see if the helicopter belonged to the Feds or if it was a news chopper, but either way its crew knew who he was and was coming after him.

He had to go to Plan B. And Plan B was a damned fine plan.

Pete buzzed down the garage door. He got out of the car, took a Styrofoam cooler from a high shelf, and brought the cooler into the house. He dismantled the doorbell and deftly rejiggered the wiring. The blasting caps were in a small taped box marked PAPER CLIPS at the back of the junk drawer. He dropped the bell ringer and one of the caps into the cooler, walked it outside to the curb, and put it next to the mailbox.

Back inside the house, Pete put another of the blasting caps into a cardboard box, covered it with a sheaf of old newspaper, and took the box out to the back porch, leaving it right outside the rear door.

He returned to the living room and peered out

through the curtains. A black SUV drove up and parked in front of his walkway. Five or six identical vehicles were now pouring onto the street from both directions. No doubt now. It was the Feds.

Pete pulled back the curtains so he was clearly visible, letting them see that he saw them. Then he plucked the kiddo out of his crib. "Let's go, stink bomb."

Stevie cried out, wriggling in Pete's arms, so Pete shook him and told him to stop. He grabbed a box of juice and a bag of Cheerios from the countertop. Then he headed out to the attached garage and got inside the car with the stink bomb on his lap.

Pete imagined the chatter going on between the SUV teams and a command post, which by now would have been set up a block away. As he waited in the dark of his garage, enemy troops gathering around his house, Captain Pete's mind rolled back several years to a day when he and his command had been traveling just outside Haditha.

It was the day the only person he cared about in the world had been murdered.

Chapter 92

PETE GORDON HAD been in the lead car at the head of a caravan of six vehicles transporting equipment and stores into the Green Zone. Riding shotgun beside Corporal Andy Douglas, he'd been busy on the walkie-talkie with Base Command when the world cracked open.

The explosion shocked every sense in his system, turning him deaf and smoke-blind, the concussive waves jolting his vehicle, lifting the chassis and dropping it down hard. He'd staggered out onto the chaotic roadside, his hearing coming back only to reveal the heartrending shrieks of the dying and wounded.

Working his way over the litter of smoldering

steel and rock, Pete found the last vehicle in his caravan. It had been overturned by the blast and was on fire. He saw three of his men: Corporal Ike Lennar was lying on the ground, twitching. Private Oren Hancock was holding his guts as they spilled into the dust. The other marine was Kenny Marshall, from Pete's hometown, his legs blown off above the knees.

Pete's eyes watered up now as he remembered that day.

He'd dropped beside his dear friend, ripped off Kenny's helmet, and cradled his bare head. The picture of Jesus inside Kenny's helmet appeared to shake its head as the helmet rolled on its rim. Pete had murmured empty words of comfort to Kenny, the boy who'd said he'd be ready whenever the Lord called him. Kenny had looked up at Pete—surprise in his eyes—and then the life had fled from him.

Pete had felt emptied of life himself, and then a torrent of rage flowed into that void. He tore off his shirt and covered Kenny's face, then shouted to his troops that the IED had been set off remotely by the car behind the caravan. What was left of his company, ten good men, had swarmed around the nondescript gray car and yanked open the doors.

There were two cowards in the front seat, and a woman and a child screamed in the back. Pete dragged the woman out of the car, her arms wrapped around the baby. He didn't understand what she said, and he didn't care. When the insurgents were facedown on the ground, Pete had shouted at them while aiming his weapon at the black sack of woman and baby at his feet.

"Do you love these people?" he'd screamed at the men. "Do you?"

He aimed his gun at the bitch, and she turned to look at him, her hands coming out from her shroud of a garment, palms up to stop the bullets. He fired his automatic, watching her jerk and flutter, and as she died he shot her squalling kiddo. He then turned his weapon on the enemy insurgents, but his troops tackled and disarmed him, put him down, and sat on him until he stopped sobbing.

Nothing was ever said about the incident. But in his mind Gordon still lived on the dusty road outside Haditha. It was the last time he'd had a tender feeling.

9th Judgement

The roar of the descending chopper brought Pete back to the moment. He was inside the car in his garage, the enemy all around, but he was eager for the action to commence. He patted the stink bomb's stomach, *tap tap tap,* and waited to make his move.

Chapter 93

BRADY'S CALL REACHED me at my desk at 1:30 p.m. He was shouting into the phone, telling me that our witness had blown the whole thing and that Peter Gordon was in an armed standoff with the FBI. "The bastard is holding his son hostage. Agent Benbow needs you on the scene, Lindsay. Pete Gordon says he'll talk only to you."

Jacobi hovered behind me. I brought him up to speed in ten words or less and saw the conflict in his face.

"Get going. Keep me posted," he barked. "Be careful," he shouted after us as Conklin and I left the squad room.

It took an agonizingly long time to get from the Hall through the traffic around the Civic Center and then to where Gordon lived. We passed through the cordon at the end of the street and saw a herd of black SUVs in front of a mud-brown two-story house with attached garage set back on a patch of dry lawn.

Agent Benbow flagged us down with his hand, came up to the passenger-side window, and said to me, "You've got experience in hostage negotiation?"

"Not enough," I said.

"Give it your best, Sergeant," he said. "Be his friend. Don't antagonize him. Try to get him to come out with the boy."

"What have I got to offer?"

"Whatever he wants. Once we have the child, he's ours."

Benbow held out a Kevlar vest. I put it on and took the bullhorn. I called out to Gordon, "Peter, this is Lindsay Boxer. I'm here because you asked for me and I want this to turn out right for everyone. Open the front door slowly, put your hands on your head, and come out, okay? No one is going to shoot."

There was no reply, so I tried again, varying my request. Then, taking a phone number from

Benbow, I called Gordon's home. Five rings. No answer. Then the machine picked up, and a little girl's voice said, "This is the Gordon house. Please leave a message."

I was out of moves, wondering why Gordon had even asked for me, when my own cell phone rang. I pulled it off my belt and stared at the faceplate. The caller ID was blocked, but I knew.

"Boxer."

"Well, hello, sweetmeat," said the Lipstick Killer.

Chapter 94

THE SOUND OF Gordon's voice in my ear bypassed reason and went straight to my adrenal glands. I broke into an instant sweat, feeling it roll down my sides, between my breasts, across my brow. I was having déjà vu of some of the most terrifying hours of my life, but somehow I forced myself to keep my voice steady.

"Gordon, no one wants to hurt you. We know you've got your son, and he's very important to all of us."

"He's important to you. I don't give a crap about him. Ask my wife. Odds are, he's not even mine."

"How can we all get what we want?"

"There's only one way, and it's my way.

Drop your weapon," Gordon said. "Call off the choppers. If I hear rotors, this conversation is over. My house is wired to explode. I have trip wires inside and out. There's one safe path, and it's the walkway to the front door. Come on down, Lindsay, come onnn downnnn."

I told Gordon to hold, and I briefed Benbow, who shook his head and said, "No frickin' way."

I said, "I'm not coming in, Gordon. I need you to come out with Steven. I guarantee your safety. My word of honor, no one will shoot."

"Lindsay, you want the kiddo, you have to come to me. I'll use you and the kid as a shield. We get into your car, and no one follows. If I see a gun, I shoot the kid and myself. If I hear a chopper, I shoot. If anyone breaks a window or steps on the lawn, the house blows. Do you copy?"

Benbow took the phone out of my hand and said, "Gordon, this is Special Agent Richard Benbow, FBI. I can't let Sergeant Boxer go in, but I'll come to your door unarmed and escort you to safety. Give us the child, and I'll personally drive you to Mexico. How's that for a deal?"

Benbow listened to Gordon's response, then

snapped the phone closed. "He told me he wants Boxer. Otherwise it's over and I can go fuck myself. He hung up."

There was only one option, the killer had told us. His way, or he would blow up everything, including his own child.

I took my Glock out of its holster and put it down on the grass. I asked God for protection, then headed up Peter Gordon's front walk.

Chapter 95

I KEPT MY eyes on the front door of a dreary house on an old shoe of a block that might be the last thing I'd ever see. I rapped on the door—no answer. I rapped even harder. No answer again.

What the hell was this?

I turned to look at Conklin and shrugged. Then I reached out and pressed the doorbell.

I heard Conklin shout, "No, Lindsay, NO!" and at that moment there were two loud explosions, a nanosecond apart.

The air cracked open. The ground lurched, and I was knocked off my feet. It was as if I'd been hit by a truck. I fell hard to the ground and was lost in a dense cloud of black smoke. I inhaled the bitter taste of cordite, coughing until my guts spasmed. Men shouted from the street, and there was the loud static of car radios. I heard Conklin calling my name.

I peered through the smoke and saw my partner lying fifteen feet away. I screamed, *"Richie,"* scrambled up, and ran to him. He was bleeding from a gash on his forehead.

"You're hit!"

He put a hand to his head and said, "I'm okay. Are you?"

"Fucking perfect."

I helped Rich to his feet. He put a hand on my shoulder. "Jesus Christ, Linds, I thought he'd killed us."

Fire was consuming an SUV at the curb. Injured men, bleeding from shrapnel wounds, leaned against their vehicles or slumped by the street. The intensity of the blast marks near the road told me that Gordon had planted a bomb on the sidewalk. Another bomb had gone off at the back of the house—and the home was starting to burn. Were these explosives meant to kill? Or to create chaos?

Where was Gordon now?

I heard the unmistakable grind of a garage door

rolling up behind me. I turned to see Gordon at the wheel of a blue Honda station wagon, heading out of the garage and down the driveway toward the street.

Rich pulled his nine, and I knew his wasn't the only weapon pointed toward that Honda. The house was covered, high and wide — and I was in the direct line of fire.

"*Hold your fire,*" I shouted toward the street.

I put up my hands and walked toward Gordon's car. As I stared through the driver's-side window, I found that I was looking into the face of a terrified child. Gordon was holding his son up to the glass, gun to the baby's head, using him as a shield.

The window lowered an inch, and Gordon's too-familiar voice came to me.

"Stink bomb," he said, "say hello to Sergeant Boxer."

Chapter 96

I TORE MY eyes away from the terrified little boy, whipped around toward the street, and screamed again, *"Hold your fire. For God's sake, he's got the child. Hold your fire."*

A blurred shape charged from behind a vehicle and continued in a line parallel to the street and toward the driveway. *It was Brady.* I watched in horror as he threw a spike strip down in front of Gordon's car, then took a stance at the head of the vehicle and, holding his gun with both hands, leveled it at the windshield.

Brady yelled to Gordon, *"Get out of the car. Get out of the car now."*

Gordon leaned on his horn, then called out to me, "Tell that bozo I have a gun to stinky's head. At the count of three, I shoot. One."

My voice was hoarse as I shouted, "Brady, put down your gun. He'll shoot the boy. He'll *shoot!*"

Gordon was a serial killer with a hostage. Procedurally, Brady was in the right and would probably be considered a hero for bringing Gordon down, even if Steven died.

Then Benbow backed me up.

"Brady, lower your weapon."

Brady hesitated, then did what he was told. I was moved by Benbow's humanity, even as I prayed he was doing the right thing.

Gordon said, "Lindsay? No guns. No choppers. No one on my tail. Do you copy? *Two.*"

I called out Gordon's demands toward the street, and the chopper flew out of range. I heard the squeal of rubber on asphalt, and I turned back to see Gordon's car shoot out of the driveway. He wheeled around the spike strip and rammed an SUV, knocking it out of the way, then jumped the curb and gunned the car down the street in the direction of the freeway.

Within seconds, this suburban block had been turned into what looked like a combat zone. The wails of sirens came from all directions: the bomb squad, ambulances, and fire rigs all rushed to the scene.

I made my way to the street, where Benbow was ordering air cover on the Honda.

Conklin put me on the phone with Jacobi, and I told him I was all right, but the truth was, I was dazed and breathless from the explosions, and my vision kept fading in and out.

As Conklin and I helped each other to our car, I kept seeing the red, terrified face of that small boy, screaming wordlessly through the car window.

Dizziness swamped me. I bent over and threw up in the grass.

Chapter 97

I WOKE UP in the emergency room, lying in a railed bed inside a curtained-off stall. Joe got up from the chair next to me and put his hands on my shoulders.

"Hello, sweetie. Are you all right? Are you okay?"

"Never better."

Joe laughed and kissed me.

I squeezed his hand. "How long was I out?"

"Two hours. You needed the sleep." Joe sat back down, keeping my hand in his.

"How's Conklin? How's Brady?"

"Conklin's got a line of stitches across his forehead. The scar's going to look good on him. Brady's a hundred percent okay but pissed off.

Says he could've taken Gordon out."

"Or he could've gotten me, himself, Conklin, and that baby all killed."

"You did good, Linds. No one died. Jacobi's in the waiting room. He hugged me."

"He did, huh?"

"Bear hug." Joe grinned and I laughed. I'm not sure that Jacobi has ever hugged *me*.

"Any news on Gordon?"

"By the time the air cover got up, his Honda was one of a million blue wagons just like it. They lost him."

"And the boy?"

Joe shrugged. I felt sick all over again. All that highly trained manpower, and Gordon had made fools of us all. "He's going to use Steven as a hostage until he doesn't need him anymore."

"I think he's ditched the kid by now, honey. Once he got out of there, a screaming toddler could only get in his way."

"He killed him, you mean?"

Joe shrugged. "Let's say he just dropped him off somewhere." Joe turned his eyes down.

A nurse came in and said the doctor would be

back in a minute. "Can I get you anything, sweetheart? Juice?"

"No, thanks. I'm okay."

When she'd gone, Joe said, "The whole deal was a diversion. The guy knows how to make a bomb."

"Did I set off the charge?"

"The doorbell. When you pressed the button, signals went to two blasting caps, one in a cooler at the curb. The other blew up the back of the house—what used to be a house."

"He asked for me, Joe. He demanded that I come to the door. He planned for me to detonate that bomb. Why me? Payback because he didn't get the money?"

"I think so. He's putting your face on his power struggle with the city—"

The doctor came in, and Joe stepped outside. Dr. Dweck asked me to follow his finger with my eyes. He hammered my knees and made me flex my wings. He told me that I had a gorgeous palm-sized contusion on my shoulder and that the cuts on my hands would heal just fine.

He listened to my breathing and my heart, both of which sped up as I thought about how Peter

Gordon could be anywhere by now, with or without that little boy—and no one knew where in the hell he was.

Chapter 98

I LEANED BACK in the passenger seat as Joe drove us home. Jacobi had told me to take a few days off and to call in on Monday to see if he was letting me work next week.

Joe said, "You're taking the sleeping cure, you hear me, Blondie? Once you're home, you're under house arrest."

"Okay."

"Stop arguing with me."

I laughed and turned my head so I could look at his strong profile in silhouette against the cobalt-blue dusk. I let centrifugal force hold me against the car door when Joe made the turn onto Arguello and I watched the steeples of St. John's go by. I must've closed my eyes, because I woke hearing Joe telling me that we were home.

He helped me onto the sidewalk outside our building and steadied me as I got my balance.

Joe was asking, "What do you feel like having for dinner?" when I saw what had to be an illusion. Across the street was a blue Honda wagon with a crumpled right fender.

"What's that?" I asked, pointing to the car.

I didn't wait for Joe to answer. I knew that car. Even from twenty feet away, I could see writing on the windshield. Fear shot through me as if Pete Gordon had lit a fuse under the soles of my shoes.

How did he know where I lived?

Why had he driven his car to my door?

I ran out into the Lake Street traffic, dodging cars blowing past me. I reached the Honda, cupped my hands to the glass, and peered inside. I saw the little boy lying on his side across the backseat. Even in the low light, the round dark spot on Steven Gordon's temple was a vivid red.

The psycho had shot his little boy.

He'd shot him—even though we'd done everything he asked us to do! I screamed, *"No!"* and wrenched the door open. The dome light flashed on, and I seized the child by the shoulder. The little boy's eyes opened, and he jerked away from me, screaming.

He was alive. I gibbered, "Stevie, are you okay, are you okay? Everything's going to be all right."

"I want my mom-my."

I used my thumb to wipe away the lipstick from the side of Steven's head, a mark so obscene, I couldn't bear to look at it. I took the child out of the car and swung him onto my hip, holding him tight. "Okay, little guy. Your mommy will be here soon."

Joe was leaning into the front seat. He fastened his eyes on the letters written on the windshield.

"What is it? What does it say?" I asked him.

"Aw shit, Linds. This guy is crazy."

"Tell me."

"It says, 'Now I want five million. Don't screw it up again.'"

He was going to kill more people if he didn't get the money. He'd done it before. I swayed on my feet, and Joe put his arms around me and the boy in my arms.

"He's desperate," Joe said. "He's a terrorist. Don't let him get to you, Linds. It's all bull."

I wanted Joe to be right, but the last time the city hadn't come through with the ransom money, Gordon had killed three more people.

"Don't screw it up again" wasn't a taunt. It was a threat, a loaded gun pointed at the people of San Francisco. And because I seemed to have become Gordon's connection to the rest of the world, that threat was also pointed at me.

Joe put his arm around me and led me back to his car, settling me into the backseat with Steven. He slid behind the wheel and locked the doors. I patted the boy's back as Joe got Dick Benbow on the line. I thought about Stevie Gordon's father, a homicidal maniac with nothing to lose.

Where the hell was he?

I didn't think I could sleep until he was dead.

WOMEN'S MURDER CLUB

Part Four

MONSTER

Chapter 99

JACOBI HAD PUT a meaty hand on each of my shoulders and looked into my eyes. "Peter Gordon is the FBI's problem, Boxer. You did everything you could do. The little boy is safe. Now, take a few days off. Take as much time as you need."

I knew Jacobi was right. I needed a rest, physically and emotionally. I'd gotten so bad that I jumped when the drip coffeemaker hissed.

On Sunday, Joe and I reached Monster Park halfway through the first quarter. The 49ers were trailing the St. Louis Rams, but I didn't care. I was with Joe. It was a great day to be sitting along the fifty-yard line. And, yeah, we were carrying guns and wearing Kevlar under our jackets.

A guard had to bump a couple of squatters from our pricey FBI-comped seats, but I forgot about that little skirmish as the screen pass unfolded below.

Arnaz Battle speared the slightly overthrown pass, tucked it in, and followed his blockers downfield. At the Rams' forty, he cut to the right sideline and raced, untouched, to the end zone.

I was jumping up and down. Joe grabbed me and gave me a great big kiss, five stars at least. I heard someone shout from the tier above, a loudmouth yelling over the crowd noise, "Get a room!"

I turned and saw that it was one of the squatters we'd evicted. He was loaded and he was a jerk. I yelled back, "Get a life!" And, to my amazement, the lout got out of his seat and headed down to where Joe and I were sitting.

And he stood there, towering over us.

"What do you think?" the guy shouted, saliva spraying out of his mouth. "You think because you can afford these seats, you can do anything you want?"

I didn't know what he was talking about, but I didn't like what I saw. When a guy goes bug-nuts at a sporting event, the next thing you know, a lot of other guys want in on the action.

"Why don't you go back to the seat you paid for?" Joe said, standing up. My fiancé is over six feet and solid, but he was not as big as the flabby loudmouth's three hundred pounds. "We're missing the game, and you're making the lady uncomfortable."

"What lady?" said the jerk. "I see a big-assed bitch, but I don't see no lady."

Joe reached out, grabbed the guy's jacket, and held it tight under his chin. I put my badge up to his face and said, "Big-assed cop, you mean."

I signaled to the stadium cops, who were jogging down the stairs. As the loudmouth was roughly hustled up the steps over encouraging shouts from the fans around us, I realized I was panting, adrenaline flooding through my veins all over again.

I had been a nanosecond from pulling my gun.

Joe put his arms around me and said, "What about it, Linds? As the man said, let's get a room."

"Great idea," I said. "I've got one in mind."

Chapter 100

THE CURTAINS IN our bedroom were stirring with a light breeze coming in through the cracked-open window. Joe had cooked for us, bathed us, admired my "perfect bottom," and wrapped me in terry cloth.

He wouldn't let me do a thing.

I was on my back in the center of the bed, looking up at him, huge and gorgeous in the soft light coming from the desk lamp and the streetlight outside.

"Don't move, Blondie," Joe said.

He tossed his towel over the door without taking his eyes off me. My breathing had quickened, and I fumbled with the belt that cinched my robe at the waist.

"What did I tell you, Linds? Doctor's orders. Don't move."

I laughed as he stretched out on the huge bed beside me.

"My nose itches," I said.

"I've got an itch, too."

"Okay, goofball."

"Goofball, huh?"

He turned onto his side and kissed my neck, a certain way he has of getting me from zero to sixty. I reached up to put my arms around his neck, and he put them back down. "Lie still."

He undid my robe and shifted me—and then we were both naked under the covers.

We lay entwined, facing each other, my leg hooked over Joe's hip, his arms wrapped entirely around me, my cheek in the hollow of his neck. I felt safe and very loved and had a sense of wonder that after all the ups and downs we'd weathered, we'd arrived at this wonderful state.

Joe gathered my hair and twisted it around his hand, then kissed my throat. He reached around me and pulled me closer. I made a small adjustment with my hips so that he could enter me. For a moment, I forgot to inhale. I was at the edge of a precipice, and I didn't want to stop.

"Hang on a sec," Joe said, reaching across me to open the drawer in the nightstand. I heard the crinkle of the foil-wrapped packet, and I put my hand on his arm and said, "No."

"I'm just getting dressed here."

"No. Really. Doctor's orders. Don't."

"Hon? Are you sure?"

"I'm sure."

Joe kissed me deeply and, while holding me tight, rolled us both so that I was lying on top of him. I raised myself up and folded my knees along his sides, placed my hands on his chest, and looked into his face. I saw the light in his eyes — his love for me. He put his hands on my hips, and, with our eyes wide open, we rocked slowly, slowly, no hurry, no worry.

There was no place I'd rather be.

No one I'd rather be with than Joe.

Chapter 101

I WAS AT my desk when Brenda buzzed me on the intercom. "Lindsay, there's a package downstairs for you. Kevin doesn't want to send it up without you checking it out."

I took the stairs down to the lobby and found our security guard waiting near the metal detector. He held an ordinary black nylon computer case, my name on a label, many yards of clear packing tape wound around it. I wasn't expecting a package. And I sure didn't like the look of this one.

"I ran it through the metal detector," our security guard said. "There's metal in here, but I can't make out what it is."

"Where did this case come from?"

"I was checking people through, a whole bunch of kids from the law school, looking in camera bags and so forth, and when I turned around, this case was on the table. Nobody claimed it."

"I'm calling the bomb squad, no offense," I said.

"None taken," Kevin said. "I'll get the head of security."

I was shaking again, my clothes sticking to me, my bruised shoulder throbbing. The hard crack of exploding bombs went off in my mind, and I thought about Joe saying that it was so easy to make a bomb, it was scary.

I called Jacobi from behind a marble column at the far side of the lobby and told him about the mystery case. I said that Peter Gordon probably had the skills to blow up the Hall of Justice.

"Get out of there, Boxer," Jacobi said.

"You, too," I said. "We're evacuating the building."

As I spoke, the alarm went off inside the Hall, and the head of security's voice came over the PA system, ordering all fire wardens to their posts.

The building was emptied—judges and juries

and prosecutors and cops and a floor full of jailed detainees all filed down the back staircase and out to the street. I left through the main door and listened to my heart lay down a three-four beat against my eardrums. Within seven or eight minutes, the building was cleared and the bomb truck was parked in front of the Hall.

I watched from behind a cordon of cops as a robot with X-ray plates in its "arms" rolled up the wheelchair ramp and through the front door of the Hall. Conklin and Chi came down to wait it out with me, and together we watched the bomb-squad tech, masked and swaddled in an antifrag, flame-retardant suit, walk behind the robot with his remote control.

I waited for the detonation I was sure would come. Then we waited some more. When I was at the screaming point, Conklin said, "We could be here all night."

So we went to MacBain's.

It was like an office party in there. Law enforcement personnel from all disciplines were whooping it up while waiting to hear if they had offices to go back to. I had my hand in the Beer Nuts when my phone rang.

It was Lieutenant Bill Berry from the bomb squad. "Your so-called bomb has been rendered safe."

I walked with Conklin and Chi to the bomb truck, which was now parked in the lot behind the Hall. I knocked on the door of the van, and when it opened, I took the case from Lieutenant Berry's hand.

"So, what's in it?" I asked him.

"Christmas in September," he said. "I think you're going to like it."

Chapter 102

"SOMETHING YOU'RE GONNA like," echoed Chi. "What would that be?"

"I'm hoping for puppies," I said.

Conklin held the door, and the three of us joined the throng of workers returning to their offices. We climbed to the third floor, turned right into Homicide, and crowded into Jacobi's office as he took his swivel chair and sat down heavily.

Jacobi's space was a pigpen as always, no offense to pigs. I moved a pile of folders from a side chair, Conklin took the chair beside me, knees bumping the desk, and Chi leaned against the doorjamb in his neat gray suit and string tie.

"Apparently this thing won't blow up," I said,

putting the computer case on Jacobi's desk.

"Are you going to open it, Boxer? Or are you waiting for an engraved invitation?"

"Okay, then."

I took latex gloves out of my pocket and wriggled my hands into them, then slit the tape with a shank that Jacobi used as a letter opener and unzipped the bag all the way around.

At first, I didn't understand what I was looking at. Little suede bags and small boxes and satin envelopes had been stuffed into the body of the case, and more of the same were tucked inside each of the pockets. Paper clipped to one of those pockets was a plain white envelope addressed to me.

I showed the envelope to my colleagues, then peeled up the flap and teased out a sheet of white copy paper that had been folded in thirds.

"Is it interesting?" Jacobi asked.

I cleared my throat and read the letter out loud.

" 'Hi, Sergeant Boxer. I did NOT kill Casey Dowling. All of her stuff is in here, and everyone else's stuff is in here, too. Please tell everyone I'm sorry. I made some bad mistakes because I thought I had no choice, but I will never steal again. Marcus Dowling killed his wife. It had to be him.'

"It's signed 'Hello Kitty.'"

I turned the case so that Jacobi could see me open the small packets. Unbelievable jewelry spilled into my gloved hands. Diamonds and sapphires that I recognized as belonging to Casey Dowling, Victorian brooches and pearls that had been Dorian Morley's, and other jewelry that had belonged to Kitty's other victims.

I sifted through extraordinary jewels that I'd seen pictured in Stolen Property's files, and then I noticed a two-inch-long leather box shaped like a pirate's trunk. I opened the box and saw a lumpy square of tissue paper.

I unfolded the paper, and a loose yellow stone the size of a grape winked up at me from the hollow of my palm. I was staring at the Sun of Ceylon.

"Is that it?" Conklin asked. "Casey Dowling's cursed diamond?"

Jacobi barely looked at it. He reached for his phone and hit number one on his speed dial—the chief's number. "Is Tony there? It's Jacobi. Tell him I've got news. Good kind."

Out of the corner of my eye, I saw Brady coming toward us in a hurry. He was huffing as he called out to me.

"Boxer, don't you pick up your messages? Listen, earlier today Peter Gordon's wife walked into the FBI."

Chapter 103

HEIDI MEYER SAT alone in an interrogation room, exhausted by the physical and emotional effects of trauma upon unimaginable trauma. Her world was changed. She was changed. How had she lived with Pete Gordon and never known who he was? Pictures kept coming into her mind, images of cooking for Pete, reasoning with him, trying to keep his lid on. She had given birth to his children, compensated for his shortcomings and psychic wounds. She'd slept next to him almost every night for the last ten years.

And now her husband had both literally and figuratively blown up their lives.

After Agent Benbow had interviewed her for three hours, he'd left her alone with a fresh cup of tea. Heidi thought about their interview, how she'd emptied every pocket of her memory in order to tell him whatever she knew to help him find her husband before he killed again.

She'd said that Pete had been freaky since coming back from Iraq. She'd said that he was always angry, that he scared the children, and that, yes, he kept weapons in the house and knew how to use explosives.

Heidi had shown Agent Benbow the bruises on her arms and had let a female agent take pictures of the black-and-blue blotches on the insides of her thighs.

And as she sat in the windowless room, it finally became clear to her how much Pete actually did hate her and the children, and that if he had in fact killed all those mothers and their children, it was because they were stand-ins for her and for Steven and Sherry.

She wondered where Pete was now and if he was tracking her, if he'd been watching her when she went into the FBI building, if he was waiting for her to leave. And now that she'd told the FBI everything, what was she supposed to do? Why hadn't someone told her what to do?

Heidi looked up as the door opened and Agent Benbow came back in with a tall blond woman. He introduced her as Sergeant Lindsay Boxer from the SFPD. Heidi's eyes watered. She stood and shook Sergeant Boxer's hand with both of hers.

"You're the one who found Stevie. Oh my God. I can't thank you enough."

"You're very welcome, Heidi. May I call you Heidi?"

"Sure."

Benbow left the room, and Sergeant Boxer pulled out a chair. She said, "Catch me up, okay? I haven't been fully briefed. Where are Steven and Sherry now?"

"They're with my friend Sarah Wells. We work together at Booker T. Washington High."

"And where is Sarah?"

"She's driving around, waiting to pick me up. She can't go home. Her husband... she's left him. We have no place to go. Even if my house wasn't bombed-out, I have to get far away from Pete."

"Let's just talk for a little bit," Sergeant Boxer said.

"Sure. Whatever I can tell you."

"Have you spoken to your husband since the events at your house?" Sergeant Boxer asked.

"He left me a voice mail. He said that when he was driving around, he was planning to kill Stevie, but then he saw something in Stevie's face. He said, 'He looks just like me. But you, Heidi. You look nothing like me at all.'"

"That was pretty ugly. What else did he say?"

"He said to tell the authorities that if he didn't get the five million bucks, he was going to find me and the kids and shoot us. That's when I contacted Agent Benbow. I gave him my cell phone with Pete's message still on it."

Sergeant Boxer nodded and said, "Excellent," and then asked, "Where do your parents live?"

"My mother was a single mom. She passed away five years ago. Sergeant, what am I supposed to do?"

The door to the interrogation room opened, and Agent Benbow returned. He had a precise haircut and a military bearing, but his expression was sympathetic, almost warm. He took a seat at the head of the table.

"Heidi, you've heard of the Witness Protection Programs?" Benbow said. "We want to put you and your kids in the program. You'll be given documents supporting new names, new identities, and you'll be given a new place to live."

"But I'm no good as a witness. I don't know anything."

"We've put people in the program for far less than being in Peter Gordon's sights. You have to let us protect you, Heidi. If we can find him, you'll do very well as a witness. He's demonstrated violence against you. And you can give a firsthand account of that."

Heidi's mind flooded with thoughts. Benbow was saying that, for her own protection, her life as Heidi Meyer was over. That for the safety of her kids, she had to disappear, delete her real life and start over as a new person. It was damned near inconceivable.

Only Sarah could make this bearable.

Heidi told Sergeant Boxer and Agent Benbow about Sarah Wells, her close friend and confidante, Stevie's godmother. And she was adamant. Sarah had to come into the program with them.

Benbow looked worried, maybe annoyed. "It's a risk, Heidi. If Sarah contacts her husband or reaches out to anyone she knows, she'll put you and your kids in mortal danger."

"I trust Sarah. I love her. She's my only true family."

Benbow drummed his fingers on the table, then said, "Okay. We'll take you to a safe house while we make arrangements. All of you have to leave now, Heidi. No phone calls. No good-byes. You can't take anything with you but what you're wearing."

Heidi was overwhelmed by the enormity of this imminent and complete break with her past—and with the idea of a future without Pete. What would it be like to live without fear, to be with Sarah every night and in the light of day?

They could all have full lives.

Tears filled Heidi's eyes again and spilled down her cheeks. She covered her face with her hands and let the tears come. When she could speak again, she said to Boxer and Benbow, "Thank you. God bless you both. Thank you."

Chapter 104

I WALKED WITH Heidi out to the street. She looked up at me, puffy-eyed and dazed, and said, "I don't know what to tell the kids."

"I know you'll find the words. Heidi, do you understand what happens next?"

"We spend the night at the FBI safe house in LA while arrangements are made. Then we fly out —"

"Don't tell me where you're going. Don't tell anyone."

"We're dropping off the edge of the earth."

"That's right. Is that your friend Sarah?" I asked as a red Saturn pulled up to the curb.

"Yes. There she is."

Heidi stepped away from me and leaned into

the car through the passenger-side window. She spoke to the driver, then said, "Sergeant Boxer, meet my friend Sarah Wells."

Sarah was a pretty brunette, no makeup, late twenties, wearing oversize clothes. She put a pink rubber ball down on the seat and reached across to shake my hand. She had an impressive grip. She said, "Listen, it's good to meet you at last. Thanks for everything."

There was an odd expression on Sarah's face—as though she were afraid of me. Had she had run-ins with the police?

"Meet me at last?"

"I meant, since you found Stevie."

"Of course."

Stevie was in a car seat in the back, sitting beside a little girl. The boy put the flat of his hand on the window and said gravely, "Hi, lady."

"Hey, Stevie," I said, putting my hand on the other side of the glass, overlapping his small palm. The girl announced, "Stevie is in love with you."

I grinned at the two children, then Heidi gave me an effusive and tearful hug. She settled into the car, then reached out her hand to take mine.

"Be happy," I said.

"You, too."

A black sedan pulled alongside the Saturn, and Agent Benbow leaned out of the car window. He told Sarah that he'd be in the lead. A second car positioned itself behind the Saturn, and then the three-car caravan drove away, escorting Heidi, Sarah, and the children to the next chapter of their new lives.

I hoped they were going to have good ones.

I watched until the cars were out of sight. I thought about Heidi and wondered how Pete Gordon would react to her disappearance with his children. And I wondered how in God's name we would find him before he killed again.

Chapter 105

LEONARD PARISI LOOKED particularly ragged the next morning when Yuki and I came to his office requesting a search warrant. Parisi, known as "Red Dog" for his dark-red hair and his tenacity, pawed through the pictures of approximately four million dollars' worth of stolen jewelry and a copy of the letter from Hello Kitty.

"Do you have any leads on this Kitty person?"

"She buried herself in a crowd coming through the front door. The security camera picked up the mob scene, but we couldn't see who left the case," Yuki said.

"Sergeant?"

"We have nothing on her identity," I told him. "The jewelry is at the lab. So far, we haven't found prints on anything. All we have is that Kitty returned every last piece. I think that gives her some credibility when she says she didn't kill Casey Dowling."

"What the hell do we have security cameras for?" Parisi groused.

Like the rest of us, Parisi had taken vast quantities of crap for his department's low conviction record in the face of San Francisco's rising crime rate. That would be our fault—the police, who didn't bring the district attorney's office enough evidence for them to build airtight cases.

"So that leaves us with what, Sergeant? The unsubstantiated statement of an anonymous self-confessed jewel thief that she's not a murderer? You actually think Dowling did it?"

"Kitty was adamant the two times I spoke with her, and I found her convincing."

"Never mind *her*. She's nobody. She's a ghost. What about Dowling?"

I told Parisi what we had on Caroline Henley, Dowling's girlfriend of two years. I explained that Dowling's net worth was in the tens of millions and that since a divorce would cost him plenty, there was a pretty good motive for killing his wife. I said that Dowling's story had been inconsistent. That his explanation of the sounds, the shots, whether or not his wife had called out to him, had changed over time.

"What else?"

"His hair was wet when we interviewed him right after the shooting."

"So he showered to get rid of evidence."

"That's what we think."

Red Dog pushed the folder of photos across the desk in my direction. "A shower is not probable cause. Before you search the screen legend's house and the news media gets hold of it and that gets us sued for defamation, you'd better have something stronger than the burglar says she didn't do it and Dowling took a shower.

"It's not probable cause for a warrant, Yuki," Parisi said. "It's not going to fly."

Chapter 106

I YANKED OUT my desk chair and crashed it hard into my trash can, then did it again for the satisfying effect of the clamor. I said to Conklin, "Red Dog won't ask for a warrant without a damned smoking gun."

Conklin stared up at me and said, "Funny you should say that. I was watching some old Dowling movies last night. Look at this."

Conklin rotated his computer screen around to face me.

I sat, wheeled my chair up to the desk, and looked at Conklin's monitor. I saw what appeared to be a movie-studio publicity still for an old spy flick.

"*Night Watch,*" Conklin said. "He made this

decades ago with Jeremy Cushing. Terrible film, but it was what they called 'camp.' It became a cult favorite. Check this out."

There was Dowling: black suit, sideburns, and a sun-lined squint. And he was holding a gun. "You're kidding me. Is that a forty-four?"

"A Ruger Blackhawk. It's a single-action revolver, a six-shooter," my partner said, clicking on another picture. The famous and now-deceased Jeremy Cushing was giving the gun to Dowling as a keepsake in a handshake photo op. You could almost hear the flashbulbs popping.

Conklin hit a key, and the printer chugged out hard copies of the photos. I picked up the phone and called Yuki. "Grab Red Dog before he goes anywhere. I'm coming back down."

We arrived at Dowling's magnificent mansion in Nob Hill before lunch, three cars full of Homicide cops dying to make a collar. I rang the doorbell, and Dowling came to the door in jeans and an unbuttoned white dress shirt.

"Sergeant Boxer," he said.

"Hello again. You remember Inspector Conklin. And I'd like to introduce Assistant DA Yuki Castellano."

Yuki handed Dowling the search warrant. "I went to school with Casey, you know," she said, stepping past Dowling into the vast gilded foyer.

"I don't think she ever mentioned you. Hey, you can't—"

Chi, McNeil, Samuels, and Lemke poured into the house right behind us with the determination of cops raiding a speakeasy during Prohibition. I had a flash of panic. Despite what I'd told Parisi —that Dowling would never ditch a souvenir of the last film Jeremy Cushing ever made—now I wasn't so sure.

"Wait," Dowling said. "What are you looking for?"

"You'll know it when we see it," I said.

I took the winding staircase up toward the master bedroom as the rest of my squad fanned out through the house. I heard the phone ring, then Dowling shouted, his voice throbbing with indignation.

"Well, Peyser, this is what lawyers are for. Come back from Napa right now."

I entered the movie star's room. Fifteen minutes later, there wasn't a drawer or a shelf that hadn't felt my hand.

I was pulling the mattress off the bed when I sensed more than heard another person in the room. I looked up to see a dark-skinned woman in a black housekeeper's dress.

I remembered her. The day after Casey Dowling was killed, the day Conklin and I came here to interview Marcus, this woman had served us bottled water.

"You're Vangy, right?"

"I'm an illegal alien."

"I understand. I...that's not my department. What do you want to tell me?"

Vangy asked me to follow her to the laundry room in the basement. When we got there, she turned on a light over the washer and dryer. She put her hands on either side of the dryer and pulled it away from the wall.

She pointed to the exhaust hose, a four-inch-wide flexible tube that vented hot air from the dryer to the outside.

"That's where he hid it," she told me. "I heard it rattle. I think what you're looking for is in there."

Chapter 107

WE WERE IN Interview Room Number Two, the larger of our interrogation spaces, the one with the better electronics. I'd checked the camera and made sure the tape was rolling before bringing Dowling in and offering him the chair facing the glass.

I wanted a full confession—for me, for Conklin, for Yuki, and for Red Dog Parisi. I wanted swift and certain justice for Casey Dowling. And I wanted to close the case for Jacobi.

Dowling had buttoned his shirt and put on a jacket, and he looked completely in control. I had to admire his cool, since his gun was in a clear plastic evidence bag on the table.

Conklin, too, looked completely at ease. I thought he was doing his best not to grin. He'd earned the right, but I wasn't doing high fives just yet. Dowling loved himself so much, he'd probably convinced himself that no one could touch him.

"My lawyer is on the way," Dowling said.

There was a knock on the door. I opened it for Carl Loomis, a ballistics tech at the crime lab. I pointed to the bagged gun, and he picked it up, turned to Dowling, and said, "I really enjoy your work, Mr. Dowling."

"Loomis, the ballistics test is top priority," I said.

"You'll have the results in an hour, Sergeant," he said as he took the evidence bag out of the room.

I turned to Dowling, who was showing me how nonchalant he was by leaning back in his chair, rocking on its hind legs.

"Mr. Dowling, I want to make sure you understand your situation. When the lab fires your gun, the test bullet is going to match the slugs removed from your wife's body."

"So you say."

Conklin said, "Believe this guy? Let's just book him on suspicion of murder. We've got him. He's done."

"Tell us what happened," I said to Dowling. "If you save us the time and cost of a trial, the DA will take your cooperation into consideration—"

"Oh. Cross your heart?"

"Just so you know, the DA goes home at five. That's in fifteen minutes. Your window to make a deal is closing fast."

Dowling snorted derisively, and Conklin laughed.

He went out of the room and came back with three containers of coffee, making a big show of adding milk and sugar to his cup, all the while humming the theme song from *Night Watch*. It was a catchy little ditty that had made the charts even when Dowling and Cushing's shoot-'em-up movie had bombed.

I saw something come over Dowling's face as Richie hummed. The nonchalance evaporated. The chair legs came down. Seemed to me that hearing that tune had focused Dowling as nothing else had.

Chapter 108

DOWLING'S CELL PHONE rang. He looked at the caller ID, opened the phone, and said, "Peyser? Where are you? What are you doing? Walking here?"

Dowling paused for his lawyer's response, then said, "You're useless. Useless." He snapped the phone shut and looked at his watch. It was five on the nose.

"Call the DA. I'm talking to you of my own free will," Dowling said. "I have nothing to hide. Do I need something in writing from you or the DA?"

"Nope," I said. I pointed to the camera in the corner over my head. "You're on the record."

Dowling nodded. He was on camera. A place he liked to be.

"I lied to protect Casey's reputation," he said. "Casey found out that I had a girlfriend. She pulled the gun on me. I wrestled it out of her hands, and the gun went off."

"Before or after the burglar went out the window?" I asked him.

"The burglar left. That's what gave her the idea. Casey saw an opportunity to shoot me. She grabbed the gun from the night table and started screaming at me. I tried to take it away from her, and it went off. That's the truth."

"Mr. Dowling, are you sure you want to tell it that way? Your wife took two bullets, remember? One to her chest. The other to her neck. She was naked and unarmed. There was no gunpowder stippling on her skin. That means you were standing at least five feet away. The angle of those shots is going to bear that out."

"That's not how it happened—"

"It's exactly how it happened, Mr. Dowling," I said. "Your Ruger is a single-action revolver. You had to pull the hammer each time before you fired."

I made a gun of my hand. I pulled back the "hammer" I made with my thumb. I said, "Bang."

Then I repeated the action and said, "Bang," again. "You want to try to convince a jury that was self-defense?"

"It was. It happened just like I said," Dowling insisted. He was sputtering now, a lisp coming into his speech, but he clung to his story. "She tried to kill me. I got the gun away from her and it went off. Maybe I panicked and fired it twice. I don't remember. I was frightened," he said, tears coming now. "I'm sorry," he pleaded. "I loved her. Ask anyone. I should never have cheated on her. It's hard, don't you see? Women come on to me all the time. Casey didn't understand that."

The door opened again, this time no knock, and Tony Peyser, Dowling's confident, thousand-bucks-an-hour attorney, came through the door.

"Don't say anything, Marc. What's the charge?" the lawyer asked me.

I was filled with a heady blend of fury and elation. Dowling's statement was on tape, and the prosecution would use it to tear him apart.

I didn't even look at the lawyer. I said, "Stand up, Mr. Dowling. You're under arrest for the murder of Casey Dowling. You have the right to remain silent…"

Conklin cuffed Dowling as I finished reading him his rights. Dowling was still protesting, "It was self-defense!"

"Who knows? Maybe the jury will believe you," I said, looking into a face that had struck love into the hearts of untold thousands of women. "But you know what I think? You're a bad actor. You really stink."

Chapter 109

I DON'T KNOW when I've needed a drink more. Cindy met me downstairs at half past six, and I drove us to Susie's in my Explorer. I was glad to have some time alone with Cindy, and I had a pretty juicy exclusive for her.

The rain was starting to come down pretty hard, the customary evening gale. As my wipers squeegeed the water off the glass, I told Cindy how the "bomb" dropped off at the Hall turned out to be four million in jewels.

"I think Kitty returned the jewelry because she didn't want that 'murder during the commission of a robbery' charge hanging over her head."

"What did her letter say exactly?" Cindy asked.

"Cindy, you can have the part about Kitty, but

we're charging Dowling with murder in the second. That's off the record, okay?"

"Fine," Cindy said. "I'll get another source on Dowling in the morning. Meanwhile, this is incredible. Hello Kitty returned the goods."

I grinned at Cindy as I quoted Hello Kitty's letter, then I parked as close as I could to Susie's. We both got out of the car and, squealing like little girls, ran a block through the sharp blowing rain.

Walking into Susie's is pretty much a peak experience every time. We've been coming here for years, so the place is packed with memories. The aroma of Susie's special spicy fish stew was in the air. The band was tuning up, and there was a mob of singles at the bar.

I saw Yuki sitting on a stool, and Cindy and I edged through the crowd until I could tap Yuki's shoulder. She turned and gave both me and Cindy hugs. Then she introduced us to the bartender. She shouted over the noise.

"Lindsay, Cindy, meet Miles La Liberte. Miles, these are my friends Lindsay Boxer and Cindy Thomas."

I shook hands with Miles, and as we said our

good-byes, Yuki leaned across the bar and kissed him on the lips.

She kissed him!

"I've been out of the loop for too long," I said to Yuki as we passed the kitchen on the way to the back room. "What was that I just saw?"

"Cute, isn't he?"

Yuki laughed and took menus from Lorraine, and the three of us slid into the booth. I held open the seat next to me for Claire.

"Darned cute," I said. "And how long has this been going on?"

"A few weeks."

"So is this … *serious?*"

"Yeah," she said, blushing and grinning at the same time.

"*Wow,*" Cindy said. "You kept that a *secret?*"

"Good for you, Yuki. A new case *and* a new boyfriend. A pitcher of brew, please," I said to Lorraine. "Four glasses."

"I have an announcement, too," Cindy said, clasping her hands, leaning across the table, practically falling into my lap. "Rich and I are living together."

"Whoa. That's fan*tastic,*" I said—and I felt it.

A hundred percent. "He didn't tell me."

"I wanted to be the one to tell you," she said.

The beer came along with a bowl of plantain chips, and Cindy talked about closet space and how the bed was too soft for Rich, and I thought about how long it had been—if ever—since all of us were happy at the same time. I wished that Claire was here to enjoy this.

I turned, looked over my shoulder, and saw her barreling down the narrow passageway toward our booth.

The look on her face could be described only as an eclipse of the sun. A thunderstorm was coming in.

Chapter 110

CLAIRE DIDN'T EVEN say hello.

She slid into the booth, poured a glass of beer, and said, "Sorry I'm late. I was on the medical examiner database, still trying to break the logjam in this Lipstick Psycho disaster. Edmund says I should take the pictures of those dead babies down from the board in my office, but I want to keep them up until that devil is in custody."

"Did you find anything?" I asked.

"I can't find a pattern that matches anything in any database but ours. No other mother-child shootings. No lipstick messages. The stippling pattern is unique. What is his motivation, his trigger, his problem? I don't have a clue. Cindy, could you pass the chips?"

"He says he's doing it for the money," Cindy said.

Claire nodded, then put her hand up, signaling that she still had the floor. She snacked and sipped, then picked up her thought.

"Okay. It's unusual, isn't it, Linds? A psycho motivated by money? But anyway let's consider that message Gordon wrote on the windshield of his car: 'Now I want five million. Don't screw it up again.' What's happening with that?" Claire asked me.

"The FBI has the car, and it's their case. I'm on call, but Benbow is in charge."

Cindy said, "What would happen if we came up with something? What if the *Chronicle* responds to that windshield message with an open letter to the killer, like we did before?"

"Be specific. What are you thinking?" Yuki asked.

"Say Henry Tyler writes the letter. He says, 'We've got the five million and want to set up a drop.' And he challenges the killer, kind of a 'back at ya,' and says, 'Don't screw it up again.'"

"And then what?" Yuki asked Cindy. "Another trap? How would it end any differently?"

I hoped for a trap that wouldn't involve me. I didn't know if I could do a repeat performance of that horrific day with the cell phone hanging around my neck, never knowing if or when Gordon would take the money and pop me.

But I had to admit what was demonstrably true.

I said, "You're saying that if the FBI doesn't do something soon, he's going to kill more people to make his point."

"More mothers and kids," Cindy said.

"Yep, that's what I'm thinking," Claire agreed. "I have an interesting idea, different from the last time. I think it could work."

Chapter 111

IT WAS MY third consecutive night in a surveillance van with Conklin and Jacobi. The vehicle was airless and soundproofed and connected wirelessly to two female undercover operatives near Nordstrom in the San Francisco Centre—they were pushing strollers with baby-sized dolls inside. I was listening to my designated decoy, Agent Heather Thomson, who was humming "Can't Touch Me," and Conklin was tracking Connie Cacase, an innocent-looking, street-talking twenty-year-old rookie from Vice.

There were seven other vans filled with cops from three divisions and with FBI agents, each vehicle following and tracking decoys with strollers in malls all around the city.

While the media were sounding the alarm nonstop on the Lipstick Killer, the mayor, the SFPD, and the FBI had declined to publish a message to Peter Gordon. And he had made no contact either.

Was Gordon angry? Stressed? Biding his time? Where was he?

If he was true to his pattern, he was overdue for a kill.

Our van was parked on Sutter, within striking distance of the Sutter–Stockton Garage, a block from Nordstom and two blocks from the Macy's at Union Square.

Jacobi's headset was tuned to SFPD Dispatch, and he had an open mic to Special Agent Benbow, who was parked two blocks away at a mobile command center.

Claire's plan made sense, but it was far from foolproof. We were all set to pounce but had no one to pounce on. Jacobi was checking in with Benbow when I heard shots through my headset. Heather stopped humming.

"Heather!" I called into my mic. "Speak to me!"

"Was that gunfire?" she asked.

"Can you see anything?"

"I'm on Stockton. I think the shots came from the garage."

I shouted to Jacobi and Conklin, "Gunfire! Agent Thomson is fine. Richie, do you have Connie? Is she okay?"

"Connie's good."

"I don't know what the hell happened, but something bad. Stay tuned," I said to Jacobi.

I struggled into my vest, made for the back of the van, swung the doors open, and exited at the rear. Conklin was right with me.

Had Peter Gordon surfaced?

If so, what had he done?

Chapter 112

PETE GORDON HAD stalked the woman through the store, watching her cover her kiddo with a blanket up to its chin before she stepped out with the stroller into the cool of the night.

His target was no beauty queen, but she had some mesmerizing tail action, a nice jiggle and sway. Pete gave her a name, Wilma Flintstone, which was perfect. Dotty little dress, hair twisted up, and Pebbles in the stroller. Wilma placed her handbag in the baby carriage and stepped off the curb, heading for the garage at Sutter and Stockton.

Pete knew that garage. It was huge, tons of indoor parking, several stories with an open top floor, visible to the high-rises all around. He was maintaining a steady ten-foot distance between Wilma and himself, keeping his eye on a cluster of security guards on the corner, when a family of four jackasses got behind Wilma and consumed his safety zone.

Pete hung back. He lowered the bill of his cap and, following his target into the garage, kept to the narrow footpath that skirted the ramp. The family blocking his sight line peeled off—and Pete picked up the pace, searching the rows of parked cars for Wilma in the dotty dress.

There were pedestrians all around, the coughs of engines starting up, the squeal of rubber as vehicles cruised down the incline. Pete was starting to worry that he'd lost her when her dress jumped out at him. She was shoving the stroller into the elevator.

The doors closed behind her and the lights above winked upward, then paused on three. Pete moved quickly to the stairs, loping up two flights, not even breathing hard as he reached the third floor.

Drivers browsed the aisles for empty parking spots, but there was no foot traffic around him. Pete brushed his hand across the gun tucked in his waistband, rounded a stanchion, and got a good straight-on look at Wilma.

And she saw him.

Wilma's face radiated alarm. She stared, bug-eyed, for a long moment, then wrenched the stroller around and ran toward her car, wheels making a frantic *whick-whick* sound.

"Miss," Pete called out. "Could you hang on a minute?"

Wilma shouted over her shoulder, "Stay away from me. Stay *away*."

Wilma had made him, but there was nowhere for her to go, handicapped as she was by her kiddo.

"Lady, you've got it wrong. My cell phone died. Look."

Her back was up against her VW Passat, one hand on the stroller's handlebars, mouth hanging open as she looked everywhere for help. The kiddo let out a scream, and Wilma reached into the stroller, and when she straightened up, Pete saw a .22 pointing at him.

He pulled his gun, but it snagged on his shirt. The muzzle was coming up when he heard the shot and felt the punch to his right shoulder. His gun jumped out of his hand and clattered to the concrete floor.

He yelled, *"Stupid bitch!"* and dove for the weapon. A slug pinged into the floor an inch from his nose. He rolled onto his back with his gun in his left hand.

"Don't move, Wilma," he said, taking aim. But his vision was blurring and lights swooped around him. He squeezed off a few rounds, but he didn't drop her. Wilma was firing again.

She kept firing.

Chapter 113

I WAS RUNNING up Sutter, Jacobi shouting into the cell phone at my ear, *"It's not one of ours!"*

"Say again."

"None of our people are involved. We got a nine one one call. Shots fired in the Sutter–Stockton Garage. Third floor."

I called ahead to Conklin over the shrill wail of sirens. We were yards from the garage and then we were inside, our feet striking metal treads as we bounded up the stairs with weapons drawn.

We cleared the doorway to the third floor, and I heard a baby screaming. I ran toward that sound. A woman in her twenties was frozen in place, standing only yards from a man lying spread-eagled, faceup on the floor. She was holding a gun.

I approached the woman slowly, leading with my badge, and said, "I'm Sergeant Boxer. It's okay now. Please hand me your gun."

"It's him, isn't it?" she said, still transfixed, her baby screaming behind her. "The coroner said to carry a gun, and I did it. It's him, isn't it? It's the killer, isn't it?"

I had to holster my weapon, shake the shooter's wrist, and pry up her fingers until I'd secured her .22. Yards away, Conklin kicked a gun out of the limp hand of the man on the floor.

I joined Conklin and put my fingers on the downed man's carotid artery.

"Rich, I've got a pulse."

Conklin called for an ambulance, and cruisers screamed up the ramp. I couldn't look away from Peter Gordon's face.

This was the monster who'd executed nine people, five of them children, a killer who'd tormented his family and held an entire city hostage.

His blood was pumping onto the concrete floor.

I didn't want to lose him. I wanted to see him in an orange jumpsuit, shackled to the defense table. I wanted to hear his fucked-up view of the world. I wanted him to pay with nine consecutive life sentences, one for each of the people he'd killed. I wanted him to *pay*.

I pressed my hand to the well of blood pumping from his femoral artery. I nearly jumped when Gordon opened sleepy eyes and turned them on me, saying, "Sweet...meat. I think...I'm shot."

I leaned so close to his face, I could almost feel a breeze as he opened and closed his eyes.

I said, "Why'd you kill them, you son of a bitch?"

He smiled and said, "Why not?" Then he exhaled a ragged breath and died.

WOMEN'S MURDER CLUB

Epilogue

911

Chapter 114

IT WAS SEPTEMBER 25, and Joe and I were having friends over to toast one another and the good days ahead.

A ham was in the oven, baking under a peppery mango glaze. Martha was begging for a taste and got a Milk-Bone instead. I was wearing a kimono and an avocado mask as I peeled the potatoes and Joe sliced apples for the cobbler. The 49ers were playing the Cowboys, the cheers of the crowd coming over the TV, when Joe's cell phone rang.

I said to him, "Don't answer that, honey."

I wasn't joking, but he grinned at me and picked up the phone.

I hadn't had a call in weeks that hadn't sent me down a tunnel of horror, and frankly I was so strung out from my job, I couldn't take even a lightbulb burning out. Or a broken fingernail. Or even a dip in the temperature. I just couldn't take it anymore.

Joe brought the phone into the living room, and I rinsed the potatoes and put them on to boil. I was in the bathroom washing avocado off my face when Joe said my name. I shut off the water and patted my eyes with a fluffy towel, and when I turned, I saw Joe looking at me, gray-faced and grim.

"There's a plane full of people on the tarmac at Dulles International," he said. "There's a guy on board, used to be an informant of mine years back. He smuggled C-four in with his hand luggage. He's threatening to blow up the plane."

"Oh my God. And the Feds want you to advise them?"

"Not exactly. The guy with the C-four, Waleed Mohammad, wants to talk to me and only me."

Joe had been deputy director of Homeland Security when we met and had become a high-level security consultant when he moved here from DC—a consultant who worked from *home*.

"So you need to call the guy," I said. "Talk him down."

"I have to fly to Washington," Joe said, walking to me, enfolding me in his arms. "A car's picking me up. I have to go right now."

It felt like my heart stopped in its tracks.

It was stupid, but I just wanted to bawl in Joe's arms and tell him he couldn't go, and if he did, I'd keep crying until he came back.

"Do what you have to do," I said.

Chapter 115

I WAS DRESSED by the time Yuki and Miles arrived. Miles, that too-cute-for-words bartender, presented me with a bottle of wine, telling me about its special qualities. I barely heard him, but I'm pretty sure I thanked him. Yuki asked where Joe was, and I told her with my voice catching, my eyes watering up, that he had rushed off to Washington.

I turned away so she wouldn't have to endure my disgraceful wet-eyed funk. So she followed me into the kitchen and helped me plate the olives and cheese. "What's going on, Lindsay?" she asked me.

"Don't look at me. It's just that everything finally got to me. You know. Everything."

"When's Joe coming back?"

I shrugged and the doorbell rang, Martha yelping happily when I opened it to Edmund and Claire. Claire surrounded me in a big hug and smothered me with flowers.

Edmund said, "Lindsay, you look gorgeous in red. Gorgeous in any way, but red's definitely your color."

Edmund joined Miles in front of the TV, the two of them having a football bonding moment as Claire went into the kitchen and poked around for a vase.

When Cindy and Rich showed up, I realized it was the first time I'd seen them together on a date. And maybe it was the first time they'd really been out in the world publicly. That their debut was happening at my home was pretty cool. I told them that Joe was MIA and why.

Rich said, "You want me to pick out some music, Linds?"

"Thanks. That would be great."

Richie was digging through the CDs and I was pulling the ham out of the oven when the phones rang, each of them, one in all four rooms ringing together.

"Are you getting the phone?" Claire asked me.

"Phones are no friends of mine."

"Could be Jacobi."

"He'd call me on my cell."

My mobile rang from my handbag. I reached in and looked at the caller ID. I didn't recognize the number. Maybe, I thought, it was coming from Jacobi's mystery date's phone.

"Warren, are you lost?"

"Sergeant Boxer?"

"Yes. Who is this?"

"This is Commander John Jordan. I'm afraid there's been an incident. I wanted to reach you before you heard it on the news."

My mind skittered like a needle across an old-fashioned vinyl record. This couldn't be about that hostage crisis in Washington. Joe couldn't have gotten there — not yet. His plane had just lifted off. I looked at the television set through the wall opening to the living room.

Talking heads had replaced the football game, and I read the breaking-news banner: CHARTER JET DOWNED IN CALIFORNIA.

Chopper footage came on, showing a green valley blemished by airplane wreckage and a blooming column of black smoke.

The commander was speaking to me, but I didn't really hear his words. I already got it. Joe's plane had gone down. They didn't know what had happened, why it had blown up or simply crashed.

The lights faded to black, and I went down.

Chapter 116

I SWAM UP out of the darkness, hearing Claire talking to Cindy, feeling something cold on my forehead, Martha's paws on my chest. My eyelids flew open. I was looking up at the ceiling of my bedroom.

Where was Joe?

Claire said, "I'm here, baby. We're all here."

"Joe? Is Joe . . . ?" I wailed. "Oh no. Oh God no."

Claire looked at me helplessly, tears rolling down her face. Cindy grabbed my hand and Yuki cried, paced, and cried some more.

I was overwhelmed with a horrible emptiness, a pain so deep, so shocking, I wanted to die. I rolled onto my side so I couldn't see anyone and covered my head with a pillow. Sobs poured out of me.

"I'm right here, sugar," Claire said.

"Tell everyone to go home. Please," I said.

She didn't answer me. The door closed, and I took Joe's pillow in my arms and rocked myself into a sleep that was more falling down a bottomless hole than floating in a dream.

I woke up not knowing why I was drowning in dread.

"What time is it?" I asked into the pillow.

"It's almost five," Claire said.

"In the afternoon?"

"Yes."

"I've only been out for an hour?"

"I'm going to get you something to put you out," she said. "I called in a prescription."

I pulled the blanket over my head.

I came up from the deep again, this time into a roar of voices, cheers—*What the hell? Was I still dreaming?* The bedroom door opened, and lights blazed. Joe was standing over me.

I screamed his name.

Was it really him? Was it? Or had I gone insane?

439

Joe opened his arms, and I threw myself against him, feeling the wool of his jacket scrape my cheek, hearing his voice saying my name.

I pulled away and looked again to be sure, and now the room was filling with my friends, standing-room only.

"I'm okay, I'm okay, sweetheart. I'm here."

I was crying again, and I was asking Joe to tell me what had happened.

"I was at the airport," Joe said. "Ours—SFO—when I got a call from my contacts in Washington saying that the passengers on that plane had overpowered Waleed. It was all over. I could go back home.

"I was arranging a car. I didn't know about that jet going down, Lindsay, until my driver turned on the radio and told me the news."

I was helped out of the bedroom and brought to the table. Joe sat beside me. The food was rubbery and cold, and it was the best damned meal I'd eaten in my life—in my whole entire life.

Wine was poured. Toasts were made. I looked around the table, and it finally sank in—Jacobi wasn't there.

"Rich, did you hear from Jacobi?"

"He hasn't called," Rich said.

We raised a glass to Jacobi's new girlfriend. We ate Joe's apple cobbler with gusto and, by the way, the 49ers won. I was weak from emotion and didn't even try to stop people from clearing the table.

By eight o'clock, I was in bed for the night with my arms wrapped around Joe.

Chapter 117

THE TELEPHONE RANG several times that night and the next morning, too. I told Joe that if he picked up a phone, he was a dead man, and then I pulled out the cord to the landline, put both our cell phones in the wall safe, and changed the combination.

Joe and I took Martha for a run, and when we got back, Joe made ham-and-cheese omelets with leftovers. It was after noon, so we opened the wine Miles had brought, Joe sipping, looking at the bottle, and saying, "Wow."

We had bought, but never had had the time to watch, the complete season-one set of *Lost*, so we pulled up armchairs to the TV and went through six episodes, broke for pizza and beer, and watched the news. We learned that the downed plane hadn't been sabotaged. The cause was pilot error, terrible enough because four people had died but a relief in that it hadn't been a failed attempt on Joe's life.

We soaked up another five hours of *Lost,* and I suppose some would say it was a waste of a day, but Joe, beer, and fantasy TV, in that order, were what I needed. I fell asleep in Joe's arms watching a recording of Bill Maher on the *Late, Late Show with Craig Ferguson.* I turned off the television and shook Joe awake.

"Huh?"

"I love you," I said.

"Of course you do. I love you, too. I wish there was a better, more expressive way to say it. Too bad you can't slip into my skin and *feel* how much I love you."

I laughed.

Boy, did it feel good to laugh.

"I believe you, sweetheart," I said.

When I woke up again, it was morning. I took Martha for a walk, and when we returned, I watched Joe sleep as I dressed. I plugged the phones back into their sockets and slugged down a glass of orange juice.

I strapped on my gun, opened the safe in the closet, and took out our cell phones. I put Joe's on the night table and gave him a kiss.

He opened his blue eyes.

"How're you feeling, Blondie?"

"Never better," I said. "Call me later."

Martha got into bed with Joe, and I went out to my car, remembering as I got into the front seat to check my phone messages.

I'd missed four calls, all of them from Jacobi. I was alarmed and swamped with guilt. I love Jacobi. Love him like the father I wished I'd had. What happened to him? How badly had I let him down?

I pressed the buttons and listened to Jacobi's first message.

"Boxer," he said, "I'm sorry not to be at your dinner party, but I've been in lockdown at the Hall with Tracchio and the mayor. This is the bottom line: Tracchio has had enough. He's resigning and I'm moving up to captain."

I was openmouthed and peeved when the beep cut him off. So I dialed up the next message.

"As I was saying, Boxer, you can have your old

444

job back," Jacobi said, in a message he'd left several hours before.

"You'll be lieutenant again, with all the perks, ha-ha. But for damned sure you can call the shots in Homicide. I'll get you more manpower, I promise you that. If you don't want the job, I'll give it to Jackson Brady. You have first call, but you have to let me know right away. The chief is making the announcement first thing Tuesday morning."

The next two calls from Jacobi were brief: "Boxer, call me back." The final one was last night. *I'd missed a deadline I didn't know I had.*

What had Jacobi decided to do? Replace himself with me? Or with Jackson Brady? Clearly I'd lost my chance to vote. I tried Jacobi's phone and got a busy signal. It happened when I called him the next time, too.

I started up my car and headed toward the Hall of Justice, but where was I really heading? I had no idea.

10th Anniversary

James Patterson
& Maxine Paetro

**Detective Lindsay Boxer finally gets married. But a missing newborn
and a series of violent attacks push the Women's Murder Club back
to full throttle before the wedding gifts are even unwrapped.**

Detective Lindsay Boxer's long-awaited wedding celebration becomes a
distant memory when she is called to investigate a horrendous crime:
a badly injured teenage girl is left for dead, and her newborn baby is
nowhere to be found. Lindsay discovers that not only is there no trace
of the criminals – but that the victim may be keeping secrets.

At the same time, Assistant District Attorney Yuki Castellano is
prosecuting the biggest case of her life – a woman who has been
accused of murdering her husband in front of her two young children.
Yuki's career rests on a guilty verdict, so when Lindsay finds evidence
that could save the defendant, she is forced to choose. Should she
trust her best friend or follow her instinct?

Lindsay's every move is watched by her new boss, Lieutenant Jackson
Brady, and when the pressure to find the baby starts interfering with
her new marriage to Joe, she wonders if she'll ever be able to start a
family of her own.

Century · London

Read on for a sneak preview of

10th Anniversary

One

THIS WAS THE DAY I was getting married.

Our suite at the Ritz in Half Moon Bay was in chaos. My best friends and I had stripped down to our underwear, and our street clothes had been flung over the furniture. Sorbet-colored dresses hung from the moldings and door frames.

The scene looked like a Degas painting of ballerinas before the curtain went up, or maybe a romanticized bordello in the Wild West. Jokes were cracked. Giddiness reigned — and then the door opened and my sister Catherine stepped in, wearing her brave face: a tight smile, pain visible at the corners of her eyes.

"What's wrong, Cat?" I asked.

"He's not here."

I blinked, tried to ignore the sharp pang of disappointment. I said sarcastically, "Well, there's a shock."

Cat was talking about our father, Marty Boxer, who left home when we were kids and failed to show when my mom was dying. I'd seen him only twice in the past ten years and hadn't missed him, but after he'd told Cat he'd come to my wedding, I'd had an expectation.

"He *said* he would be here. He *promised*," Cat said.

I'm six years older than my sister and a century more jaded. I should have known better. I hugged her.

"Forget it," I said. "He can't hurt us. He's nobody to us."

Claire, my best bosom buddy, sat up in bed, swung her legs over, and put her bare feet on the floor. She's a large black woman and funny — acidly so. If she weren't a pathologist, she could do stand-up comedy.

"*I'll* give you away, Lindsay," she said. "But I want you back."

Cindy and I cracked up, and Yuki piped up, "I know who can stand in for Marty, that jerk." She stepped into her pink satin dress, pulled it up over her tiny little bones, and zipped it herself. She said, "Be right back."

Getting things done was Yuki's specialty. Don't get in her way when she's in gear. Even if she's in the *wrong* gear.

"Yuki, wait," I called as she rushed out the door. I turned to Claire, saw that she was holding up what used to be called a foundation garment. It was boned and forbidding-looking.

"I don't mind wearing a dress that makes me look like a cupcake, but how in hell am I supposed to get into this?"

"I love my dress," said Cindy, fingering the peach-colored silk organza. She was probably the first bridesmaid in the world to express that sentiment, but Cindy was terminally lovesick. She turned her pretty face toward me and said dreamily, "You should get ready."

Two yards of creamy satin slid out of the garment bag. I wriggled into the strapless Vera Wang confection, then stood with my sister in front of the long freestanding mirror: a pair of tall brown-eyed blondes, looking so much like our dad.

"Grace Kelly never looked so good," said Cat, her eyes welling up.

"Dip your head, gorgeous," said Cindy.

She fastened her pearls around my neck.

I did a little pirouette, and Claire caught my hand and twirled me under her arm. She said, "Do you believe it, Linds? I'm going to dance at your wedding."

She didn't say "finally," but she was right to think it, having lived through my roller-coaster, long-distance romance with Joe, punctuated by his moving to San Francisco to be with me, my house burning down, a couple of near-death experiences, and a huge diamond engagement ring that I'd kept in a drawer for most of a year.

"Thanks for keeping the faith," I said.

"I wouldn't call it faith, darling," Claire cracked. "I never expected to *see* a miracle, let alone be *part* of one."

I gave her a playful jab on the arm. She ducked and feinted. The door opened and Yuki came in with my bouquet: a lavish bunch of peonies and roses tied with baby blue streamers.

"This hankie belonged to my grandmother," Cindy said, tucking a bit of lace into my cleavage, checking off the details.

"Old, new, borrowed, blue. You're good." "I cued up the music, Linds," said Yuki. "We're *on*." My God. Joe and I were really getting married.

Two

JACOBI MET ME in the hotel lobby, stuck out his elbow, and laughed out loud. Yuki had been right. Jacobi was the perfect stand-in Dad. I took his arm and he kissed my cheek.

First time ever. "You look beautiful, Boxer. You know, more than usual." Another first. Jacobi and I had spent so much time in a squad car together, we could almost read each other's minds. But I didn't have to be clairvoyant to read the love in his eyes. I grinned at him and said, "Thanks, Jacobi. Thanks a lot." I squeezed his arm and we walked across an acre of marble, through tall French doors, and into my future.

Jacobi had a limp and a wheeze, the remnants of a shooting a couple of years back in the

Tenderloin. I'd thought we were both going to check out that night. But that was then.

Now the warm, salty air embraced me. The great lawns flowed around the shining white gazebo and down to the bluff. The Pacific crashed against the cliff side, and the setting sun tinted the clouds a glowing whiskey pink that you could never capture on film. I'd never seen a more beautiful place.

"Take it easy, now," Jacobi said. "No sprinting down the aisle. Just keep step with the music."

"If you insist," I said, laughing.

Two blocks of chairs had been set up facing the gazebo, and the aisle had been cordoned off with yellow crime scene tape. POLICE LINE. DO NOT CROSS.

The tape had to have been Conklin's idea. I was sure of it when he caught my eye and gave me a broad grin and a thumbs-up. Cat's young daughters skipped down the grassy aisle tossing rose petals as the wedding march began. My best friends stepped out in time, and I followed behind them.

Smiling faces turned to me. Charlie Clapper on the aisle, guys from the squad, and new and old friends were on the left. Five of Joe's look-alike brothers and their families were on my right. Joe's parents turned to beam at me from the front row.

Jacobi brought me up the gazebo steps to the altar and released my arm, and I looked up at my wonderful, handsome husband-to-be. Joe's eyes connected with mine, and I knew without any doubt that the roller-coaster ride had been worth it. I knew this man so well. Our tested love was rich and deep and solid.

Longtime family friend the Reverend Lynn Boyer put our hands together, Joe's hand over mine, then whispered theatrically so that everyone could hear, "Enjoy this moment, Joseph. This is the last time you'll have the upper hand with Lindsay."

Delighted laughter rang out and then hushed. With the sound of seagulls calling, Joe and I exchanged promises to love and cherish through good days and bad, through sickness and health, for as long as we both lived.

Do you take this man to be your wedded husband?

I do. I really do.

There were nervous titters as I fumbled with

Joe's wedding band and it spun out of my hand. Joe and I both stooped, grabbed the ring at the same time, and held it between our fingers.

"Steady, Blondie," Joe said. "It only gets better from here."

I laughed, and when we resumed our positions, I got that gold band onto Joe's finger. The Reverend Boyer told Joe he could kiss the bride, and my husband held my face between his hands.

We kissed, and then again. And again. And again.

There was wild applause and a surge of music.

This was real. I was Mrs. Joseph Molinari. Joe took my hand and, grinning like little kids, we walked back up the aisle through a shower of rose petals.

James
Patterson

**To find out more about James Patterson
and his bestselling books, go to
www.jamespatterson.co.uk**

We support

I'm proud to support the National Literacy Trust, an independent charity that changes lives through literacy.

Did you know that millions of people in the UK struggle to read and write? This means children are less likely to succeed at school and less likely to develop into confident and happy teenagers. Literacy difficulties will limit their opportunities throughout adult life.

The National Literacy Trust passionately believes that everyone has a right to the reading, writing, speaking and listening skills they need to fulfil their own and, ultimately, the nation's potential.

My own son didn't used to enjoy reading which was why I started writing children's books – reading for pleasure is an essential way to encourage children to pick up a book. The National Literacy Trust is dedicated to delivering exciting initiatives to encourage people to read and to help raise literacy levels. To find out more about the great work that they do visit their website at www.literacytrust.org.uk.

James Patterson